I0622934

Willow City

David R. Beshears

Based on the screenplay
"Willow City"

Greybeard Publishing
Washington State

Copyright 2019 by David R. Beshears

All rights reserved. No part of this book may be reproduced or transmitted in any form or by any means, electronic or mechanical, including photocopying, recording, or by any information storage and retrieval system, without permission in writing from the publisher.

Greybeard Publishing
P.O. Box 480
McCleary, WA 98557-0480

ISBN 978-1-947231-03-0

Willow City

Willow City

Chapter One

The train passenger car was old, well-worn, well-used. Narrow, wooden bench seats faced one another, most of them occupied. The passengers wore simple clothes; some were in quiet conversation, but most were silent. There was a gentle rocking to the train car, the hollow clack-clack sound of train wheels on tracks.

Alan Thornton was sitting near a window, staring into the darkness beyond the glass. He was one of but a few passengers with a bench seat to himself. He was in his late thirties, clean-shaven, his hair military cut without being tight and high. He had the look of military without the uniform. He wore a plain, inexpensive sport jacket, a white shirt with no tie.

He turned from the window and glanced about at the passengers.

A young woman and a four year old boy were sitting on the bench directly across from him. The boy was looking at him. Alan looked casually back without comment.

The boy's mother looked from the boy to Alan, back to the boy. She leaned near her son and whispered something. The boy ignored her and continued to look blankly at Alan.

Across the aisle, a man was reading a newspaper. He looked up from his paper to Alan. His expression didn't change. He turned the page of his newspaper, refolded it and returned to his reading.

Alan looked again to the woman and the boy. Both were watching him now. He tried to ignore them, turned again to the darkness beyond the window; the sound of wheels on the tracks, the gentle rocking of the passenger car.

The door at the front of the car opened, the conductor came in. He closed the door behind him and started down the aisle. "Three minutes. Three minutes to Willow City." He continued past Alan. "Three minutes."

Passengers began moving about, preparing for their arrival in Willow City. There were no raised voices, no happy comments. The conductor reached the rear of the car and exited.

Alan looked away from the passengers and again to the darkness beyond the window.

He was in no rush.

Alan stepped down from the passenger car and onto the station platform, an olive-drab duffle in hand. He was the last one out of the train. He took a moment to look about the platform.

A drab-colored wall ran the length of the platform, narrow gate openings every forty feet with turnstiles through which passengers were passing. There were old posters on the wall, their edges torn, corners curled with age. One pictured a proud soldier welcoming fellow solders home, another encouraged joining in the defense of the Federation. All the posters were either in support of the city-state or of the national government. All had a strong authoritarian air.

There was very little conversation on the platform considering the number of people moving about. Alan walked to the nearer gate and waited in line. A heavily-armed transportation security officer stood near the turnstile, to one side of the transportation official. He studied each passenger as they inserted their ID cards into the reader before passing through.

Alan's turn came. He brought his ID card from his shirt pocket as he approached, slipped it into the card reader. When the indicator turned green, he pulled out the card.

The transportation official watched a monitor. Alan's picture and personal data displayed:

Thornton, Alan, Master Sergeant, Retired.

When a second indicator light turned green Alan continued on through the turnstile and took a set of stairs up into the station. A row of ticket cages ran along one wall, two rows of wooden benches lined the wall opposite. Tall windows and several double doors were set into the front wall directly ahead.

Two security officers watched travelers coming and going. The station was relatively quiet, voices muffled.

Alan started across the floor toward the exit. As he neared the doors, a middle-aged man came through from outside wearing a long, gray coat and shaking a wet umbrella as he readied to close it. He stepped to one side and let Alan pass.

The world outside was dark, still, quiet. The street, sidewalks and buildings all had a wet sheen from the recent rain. The air felt damp.

There were three taxis parked at the curb, the vehicles older, nondescript, high-profile sedans. Alan walked to the first taxi in line, opened the back door and tossed his duffle. He climbed in after it. A video display was set into the back of the driver's seat, an ID reader directly beside the display. Alan slipped his ID card into the slot, pulled it out when the indicator showed green.

Only then did the driver say anything, speaking to the rear view mirror.

"Where to?" he asked, no emotion.

Alan settled into the seat. "Veterans Center."

"Which one?"

"The one with the fewest fleas."

"That'd be Vet Cen 6." The driver started the vehicle. "On Broadway."

"That's fine." Alan turned his attention to the view beyond the side window.

The taxi pulled away from the curb. Alan absently watched the scene passing by as they traveled the city; dark streets with glowing globes on tall, evenly spaced lamp poles, wet brick buildings with lighted windows. There were only a handful of vehicles on the streets, most of them other taxis. There were a few pedestrians about, most wearing dark or gray coats.

The taxi slowed only slightly as it maneuvered past a police van, the rear doors open. Several bound prisoners were being roughly pushed into the back of the van. Another prisoner, at the direction of another armed police officer, was removing posters from the side of a building.

The driver turned the taxi onto Broadway, worked his way up the empty street before pulling up to the curb in front of Veterans Center 6. Alan climbed out of the back, reached back in and pulled out his duffle. He closed the door without a word to the driver, turned his attention to the building in front of him as the taxi pulled away.

The veterans center was a wide, squat three-storey building. There were several large windows along the first floor, rows of smaller, evenly spaced windows on the second and third floors.

Alan crossed the walk and entered the lobby. There was an open-space lounge to the left with a mismatched assortment of old couches, chairs, side tables and coffee tables. A television monitor was mounted on the wall.

Alan continued ahead to the front desk on the right and set his duffle at his feet. The desk clerk looked like a retired military man, though a few years of civilian life appeared to have softened him up some. He had put on a few extra pounds, but had kept his hair cropped short and his clothes neat and trim.

"Yes sir?" he asked.

"I need a room," said Alan.

The desk clerk slid a card reader across the counter. Alan took his ID card from his pocket and slipped it into the slot. When the indicator light showed green, he pulled the card out and slipped it back into his pocket.

The desk clerk looked at the display that was set behind the counter.

"Master Sergeant Thornton," he stated. "Welcome to Willow City. How long will you be staying?"

"Retired," said Alan. "A couple of weeks, at least."

The clerk moved to one side, began working at a keyboard as he looked at another monitor.

"I'll put you down for a month, with an option for more, just in case."

"That'll be fine. Thanks."

The clerk finished entering data, hit a key. He brought a plastic key card out, slid it across the counter to Alan.

"Room 304," he said. "Two flights up, but its real quiet."

Alan took the key card. He nodded acknowledgment to the desk clerk as he picked up his duffle and looked in the direction of the staircase at the far end of the lobby.

"Much appreciated," he said, starting to the staircase.

Three older veterans watched from the lounge. The television monitor on the wall was displaying a news story of a small group of unruly disruptives being collected and hauled away so that school children could continue their outing to the Willow City museum.

Alan reached the third floor and started down a wide, dimly lit hallway. The carpet was old, faded and well-worn from years of foot traffic. He reached the door with "304" displayed on it. Sliding the key card into the slot, he heard a hard click sound and pushed the door open.

The room was simple, sparse; a twin bed and bedside table, a desk and chair. A narrow door led to the bathroom. There was a small flat-screen television monitor mounted on one wall.

He tossed the duffle onto the bed and walked to the window. Pulling the curtain aside, the view was of the street in front of the center. There were evenly spaced globe lamps on tall poles. Across the street was a dark, two-storey building of brick, a handful of windows on the second floor, all dark.

Chapter Two

Come morning, Alan worked his way downstairs to the main floor. A young soldier in uniform stood at the front desk, his duffle at his feet. He was talking with the desk clerk behind the counter.

Alan turned right at the foot of the stairs, went through an open doorway and entered the phone center. The room was square, two walls lined with old phone booths of wood and glass; a handful of the booths were occupied.

A well-armed security officer was standing to one side, quietly observing all activity while appearing slightly bored.

Alan went to the nearest available booth, closed the door and sat on the small bench. He slid his ID card into the slot. The indicator light turned green, and he returned the card to his shirt pocket. He reached down and brought a small notebook from his jacket pocket. Opening it, he turned several pages until he found the page with a phone number written on it and nothing else.

He returned the notebook to his pocket, lifted the phone receiver and keyed in the number. There were two muffled rings, then a hollow click.

He heard a voice then. "Chavez."

"Alan Thornton," said Alan.

"Hello, Alan," said Chavez. "When'd you get in?"

"Last night." Alan glanced out into the phone center. Several people were walking across the room. The security officer quietly watched it all. "Are you free today?" he asked.

"I can be," said Chavez. "Six o'clock?"

"That's fine. Gray Swan."

"Six, then. See ya', Alan."

"Chavez." Alan placed the receiver back in the cradle. He took a moment, then opened the door and slid out of the booth.

The security officer eyed Alan, his focus drifted then to another of the phone center customers.

Alan left the phone center, took the short side hall to the Vet Center's cafeteria. It was small for a cafeteria, with eight tables scattered about the room, half of them occupied, veterans eating their breakfast in silence.

A self-serve buffet counter was set along the back wall. A drink dispenser was set against the right wall next to a counter with silverware, glasses and napkins.

Alan worked his way across the room to the buffet. He took a tray from the stack, grabbed a plate. Working his way along the buffet, he spooned up a serving of scrambled eggs and grabbed two pieces of toast. He placed a fork and napkin on his tray and walked to an empty table.

He ate in silence, glanced now and then at those at the other tables, but other than that he kept to himself.

He looked up again, briefly, when someone new came into the cafeteria. He ignored the man as he approached his table and rested a hand on the back of the chair across from him.

Cavanaugh appeared calm, confident. He was in his thirties, dressed casual but not inexpensive. His hair was well-groomed, combed back from a high forehead.

"Master Sergeant," he said calmly. "Mind if I sit down?"

Alan kept eating, but indicated the chair.

"Retired," he stated.

"If you say so." Cavanaugh pulled out the chair and sat down. "The name's Cavanaugh. I wanted to drop by and welcome you home."

"Thanks." Alan scooped up another forkful of scrambled eggs. "How's Cain holding up these days?"

Cavanaugh smiled at Alan's observation.

"Mr. Cain is doing quite well. He sends his best."

"Uh, huh," Alan managed. "Tell him I said hi."

"I'll certainly do that." Cavanaugh leaned forward then, rested his arms on the table. He clasped his hands. "Mr. Cain would also like you to know that if there is anything he can do to help you with your endeavor, you have but to ask."

"Is that so?" Alan took another bite of scrambled eggs. "Cain could save me a lot of trouble. A few answers, maybe point me to where I need to go."

"Mr. Cain doesn't have your answers, Sergeant Thornton." Cavanaugh slid his arms from the table, leaned back in his chair. "But I can assure you that if he can open a door, perhaps clear a path—"

"I have but to ask," finished Alan.

"Exactly." Cavanaugh took a sharp breath, gave a half-smile. He slid his chair back and got to his feet. "Again, welcome home."

Alan used his fork to draw the last of his scrambled eggs into a pile, scooped up the forkful.

"Thanks." He shoveled scrambled egg into his mouth. "I might just take Cain up on his offer."

Cavanaugh nodded acknowledgment and good-bye. Alan picked up a piece of toast and took as bite as he watched him leave the cafeteria.

The desk clerk stepped up to the counter when Alan stepped from the staircase and approached the front desk.

"Good afternoon, Sergeant Thornton. How is your room?"

"Very quiet, as you said," said Alan. "How can I get a cab?"

The desk clerk reached for the phone behind the counter, picked up the heavy receiver.

"One quick call," he stated.

"Thanks." Alan moved away from the counter and started toward the front door.

Outside, evening gray would soon be giving way to dark. Alan waited at curb, stood patiently, looking patiently up and down the street. A police vehicle passed slowly by, the officer in the passenger seat eyeing Alan with indifference.

It was several minutes more before a taxi appeared, approached the veterans center and pulled up before Alan. He opened the back door of the cab and climbed into the back seat. He slipped his ID card into the reader, pulled it out when the indicator turned green.

He spoke to the cabbie as he slid back in the seat. "The Gray Swan."

The outside of the nightclub was little more than a plain wall with a simple door. Above the door was a simple sign that read "The Gray Swan".

The taxi came slowly around a corner and pulled up to the curb in front of the nightclub. Alan climbed out, closed the door. The taxi pulled away as Alan walked toward the nightclub door.

Entering the nightclub, the Gray Swan was narrow and deep. Booths lined one wall, a bar lined the other. There were several dozen tables on the floor, with a stage at the far end, raised about a foot and a half above the club floor.

Carl Underwood was sitting at a piano to one side of the stage, tickling the ivories without really playing.

Carl was forty five years old, African American with close-cropped hair that was graying at the temples. Hard-rimmed glasses sat on his large nose. He held a cigarette between his lips; the ashtray atop the piano was half-filled with ash and butts.

Other than Carl there was only Eddie, standing behind the bar, and two men sitting at one of the tables nursing their drinks. The place was open for business but things wouldn't begin to pick up for another hour.

Carl looked out across the room, watched Alan cross the club floor to the bar. He gave Alan a nod when Alan looked in his direction, continued working the piano keys, watched absently as Alan placed an order with the bartender.

Carl's sister Bonnie Harper walked across the stage and leaned against the piano. She was in her forties but a hard life was reflected as wear-and-tear on her face. She was wearing a dressing gown, as if she were partially dressed for the evening's show.

Carl glanced briefly up at his sister, noted that she saw Alan standing at the bar waiting for his order.

"He just came in," he said, returning to his piano keys.

"So I see," said Bonnie. "He shouldn't have come back."

"Come on, sis. What choice did he have?"

Bonnie watched Alan turn from the bar, tall glass in hand, and walk across the floor toward the row of booths. "Five'll get you ten that Cain already knows he's here," she said.

"Ten'll get you twenty Alan knows that." More tickling of the keys; he stopped then and looked over at Alan, who was just sliding into a booth. "He's here to find his brother. Arthur Cain may be able to help."

"Oh, I expect Arthur Cain knows exactly where Richard is buried." Bonnie pushed away from the piano, on her way backstage to finish getting ready for the evening's shows.

In the booth, Alan took a long drink from his glass, watched Bonnie Harper leave the stage. He looked over then to Carl. Carl gave Alan a slow nod, returned his focus to tickling the ivories.

As the late afternoon drew nearer to early evening, activity in the club slowly picked up, though it remained fairly quiet. The pair of men at the table in middle of the floor continued talking back and forth. Now and then someone new entered the club; a woman went to the bar, a couple settled at a table near the stage. Carl continued working at the piano.

Chavez slid into the booth opposite Alan.

"Alan... long time, my friend. You look good." Chavez was Hispanic, in his late thirties. He had a dark complexion and dark hair, was husky but not overweight. He was dressed in khaki pants, a button shirt and light jacket.

"Good to see you, Chavez." Alan took another drink from his glass. "How's the wife and kid?"

"Keepin' outta trouble," said Chavez with a shrug.

"That's as good as it gets, these days."

"Can't expect more, my friend." Chavez looked across to the bartender. He caught his attention, and that was all it took. Eddie nodded, took a mug and began pulling a draft.

Chavez indicated Alan's glass. "Still with the iced tea, eh?"

"Never ran across a reason to change," said Alan.

"The war," Chavez stated flatly.

"I'm done with that," said Alan.

"Yeah... so I hear," said Chavez. He leaned back to allow the bartender to set the beer mug on the table. "Thank you, Eddie."

Eddie winked conspiratorially to Alan as he responded to Chavez.

"Booth service costs you extra, Chavez."

"Ah... and so explains the gross miscalculation on my tab."

Eddie gave another look to Alan before turning from the booth.

"Don't let this guy lead you astray, Thornton," he said.

"That's gonna be tough, Eddie," said Alan. "The man just oozes trust."

"I see that... the aura is blinding."

Chavez half-grinned at the departing Eddie and took a swallow from his beer.

"Done your twenty and out, eh?" he asked Alan, setting the mug back on the table.

"I'm done with that," repeated Alan.

"I get ya'," said Chavez, a bit darkly. "It never was what they said it was."

There was an uncomfortable pause, then. Alan's attention drifted out across the nightclub. Another group was settling in at a table near the stage.

Chavez took another drink from his beer.

"You home for good, then?" he asked.

"Depends."

"Right," sighed Chavez. "That."

"That."

"It could be difficult, my friend. What you're doing, what you're looking to do, is most inconvenient for those who thought the matter closed."

"They thought wrong." Alan looked down at his iced tea, turned the glass about, took a drink. "So what happened to my brother?" he asked.

"Sorry, man. I don't know." Chavez indicated the nightclub. "He was here that night. Disappeared sometime after that."

"Who do you think *disappeared* him?"

Chavez shrugged. "He'd been pissing in the mayor's cereal for two years. Could be the city-state."

Alan watched several newly arrived customers move past the booth on their way to another.

"What about Arthur Cain?"

"Possible, I suppose," said Chavez. "Richard didn't make many friends there, either."

"I've already had a visit," said Alan. "Offering to help."

"No doubt. You take him up on it?"

"It's an option."

Chavez frowned, shook his head. "Cain, the Mayor, Chief Archer... interesting bedfellows. A complicated relationship."

"I might be able to use that."

"Tread carefully there. That relationship has been strained of late."

Alan only nodded at that. He didn't really know how he might use that situation to accomplish his goals in any event. It was something, though, to put on the shelf to bring down later.

Chavez watched Alan a moment, took another drink from his beer.

"It's really great to see you again, Alan, but I'm not sure what I can do to help. The city has only gotten darker since your last visit. I've mostly been laying low. What connections I had, what feeds I had, long gone or outright dead."

A waitress made an appearance out on the floor, stood at a table ready to take an order. Several more customers entered the nightclub.

"I gotta think of the family," Chavez finished.

"I get it. It's cool." Alan lifted his glass. "I'll dust off a few of my own old connections, see if any of 'em are still breathing."

"Other than me?" Chavez smirked. "You got connections other than me?"

Alan ignored the comment. He took a cautious look about them.

"I could use a weapon," he stated. "Couldn't bring anything into the city."

"That won't be easy."

"I don't want you to put yourself in Archer's headlights."

"No." Chavez hesitated. "I may know someone. Give me a couple of days."

Alan considered. "A couple of days should be about right."

"You plannin' on walkin' into something where you need a gun?"

"Not at all," said Alan in a flat tone.

Chavez studied Alan's blank expression for a long moment.

"Yeah," he said at last, rather cautiously. "I can't promise anything, but I might be about to come up with something."

Bonnie Harper appeared on the stage then, fully dressed for her show. She walked over to Carl at the piano; they fell into conversation.

Chavez finished off his beer, slid out of the booth.

"Gotta run," he said. "Vet Center 6, right?"

"Room 304."

Chavez rested a hand on Alan's shoulder as he passed him on his way out. "Watch yourself, my friend."

Alone again, Alan settled back, watched as Carl and Bonnie made preparations to start their first set.

He took a final swallow of his tea then, looked across at the waitress standing beside a nearby table. When she looked his way, his lifted the empty glass. She nodded acknowledgment.

Up on the stage, Bonnie moved to the microphone, looked out across the nightclub floor.

"Good evening, everyone," she said. "What say we get this started?"

There was a light clapping from the audience, which was still somewhat sparse.

"All right, then." Bonnie looked in Carl's direction, and he began working the keys. Bonnie turned again to the audience, repositioned the microphone, and began a classic, smoky, 40s song in the film noir style...

Several hours later, the overhead lights were dimmed, most of the tables and booths were occupied. Alan was alone in his booth, leaning back, one arm resting on the table, the other on the back of the booth seat.

On the stage, Bonnie stood at the microphone, a soft-lit spotlight on her. She was in the midst of another song as Carl backed her at the piano. When they finished, the audience clapped appreciatively and the house lights came up.

"Thank you, ladies and gentlemen," she said. "My brother Carl and I will be taking a short break, but we'll be back for the second set before you know it. Don't you be going anywhere."

She nodded another thank you, took a step back and turned to walk over to the piano to a second round of light clapping. She took the cigarette from Carl, drew on it, then handed it back and breathed out a cloud of smoke.

Alan shifted position as she stepped off the stage and walked in his direction. He leaned forward and placed his forearms on the table as she slid into the booth opposite him.

"Bonnie," he said. "You sound great."

"Thanks." She pulled Alan's glass of tea across the table, took a swallow, and slid it back. "What the hell are you doing here, Alan?"

"Listenin' to bluesy jazz."

"You don't do cute very well."

"Good to see you, too."

Bonnie frowned then, took a slow breath and studied Alan.

"I've missed you," she said at last. "Now get your ass out of town."

"I can't do that," Alan stated calmly.

"You won't find your brother. You'll just end up dead. Hell, ya' got the mayor and police chief on one side, Arthur Cain on the other, and you're not exactly on the best of terms with either."

"So long as neither's the cause of whatever happened to Richard, I got no quarrel with either."

Bonnie slid forward, leaned over the table.

"The last time you were in town," she said, "you called the mayor a tyrant and Cain his flunky."

"Okay, I was wrong on that," Alan said, smirking. "The mayor's the flunky."

"Damn it, Alan. You stirred up a lot of crap. And you're only gonna make things worse coming back looking for Richard."

"And you really think I can let this go..." Alan's words were a cool statement.

"What's to let go? I'm sorry. He's gone."

Alan grasped his glass as he leaned in close. "Whatever happened to Richard, I will know who is responsible."

Bonnie reached out and placed a hand on Alan's arm. Carl approached the booth and Bonnie looked to him for support as he slid in beside Alan.

"Yeah, we kinda' figured that," she said.

Carl nodded curtly. "About time for the next set, Sis."

Bonnie gave a slow nod in response, looked warmly across at Alan, still holding his arm.

"It really is good to see you." She leaned back and slid out of the booth.

Carl spoke to Alan as he watched his sister walk back to the stage.

"Times are bad right now, Alan. The mayor's really clamping down. Laws changing, policies; and he's got the chief black-booting all over town."

From all that Alan had heard, and in some cases had witnessed, it was the same with the other city-states.

"What about Cain?" he asked.

"Arthur Cain's a whole other story," said Carl. "The syndicate is as strong as it ever was, but he's still gotta dance the tune with city hall."

"I understand there's a bit of strain there."

"You could say that. Something'll give soon, and when it does... it's gonna get ugly 'round here." He slid out of the booth then, held a hand out to shake hands. "Gotta get back. Good to see you, Alan."

"Thanks, man."

They shook hands, and Carl leaned in close.

"I got someone who might be able to help. She'll be at Sally's at ten." He pulled back, gave Alan a pat on the shoulder. "Enjoy the show, my man."

The night was dark, damp and a bit muggy. The asphalt streets and brick walls shone with damp. A car passed, a few moments later another. Alan approached the intersection; Sally's Café was on the corner across the street, large windows facing the cross streets.

What appeared to be an unmarked police car was parked across from the café. Two people were sitting in the front seat.

Alan crossed the intersection, looked in through the windows and noted the few customers in the café before entering.

Booths lined the exterior windowed walls, a lunch counter ran the length of the café. Two of the stools at the counter were occupied, and a group of men were sitting in a booth at the far end of the café.

A woman in her thirties was sitting alone in a booth near the door. Her thick, blonde hair fell in waves to her shoulders. Her dark eyes always seemed to be in shadow, creating an air of the femme fatale.

Alan slid into the booth opposite the woman. She hardly looked at him, pointedly ignoring him. She took a long sip from her coffee, set the cup onto the saucer with a soft clink sound.

Alan waited for some acknowledgment from her. She looked at him briefly, but said nothing.

"Valerie Baker?" he asked.

"Who's asking?" she asked.

"Alan Thornton."

Valerie studied Alan a moment.

"I see the resemblance," she said at last.

"You know Richard?"

Valerie slowly lifted her cup and took another sip of her coffee.

"I knew him," she said.

The waitress came to the table. She held a pad and pencil and looked expectantly at Alan. He glanced up at her, then past her at a glass display case behind the counter.

"Coffee and apple pie." He took his ID card and handed it to her.

"You got it."

Valerie looked side-glance at the receding waitress.

"That a valid ID?" she asked Alan.

"Yes."

"Then they're tracking you."

The barest hint of a grin. "I expect that's so."

Valerie thought that comment over for a moment, realized what he was saying.

"I see. You watch yourself, Mr. Thornton."

"I'm hearing that a lot lately." Alan straightened, leaned a bit closer to the table. "What happened to my brother?"

Valerie took another sip of her coffee, set the cup back onto the saucer. She looked dispassionately across to Alan.

"I don't know."

Alan stared back. "I was told you could help," he stated flatly.

"And just what is it that you need help with, Mr. Thornton?"

"I want to know what happened to my brother."

"And?"

"And hold those responsible to account."

"Good luck with that." There was a moment's hesitation. "You're certain something bad happened..."

"Are you saying different?"

"Not at all. I know something bad happened. But what makes you think so?"

"Because he's disappeared and nobody can tell me where he's gone. Can you?"

The waitress returned then with a slice of pie, a coffee cup and a carafe of coffee. She filled Alan's cup, then refilled Valerie's. She set Alan's ID card beside his plate of pie.

Valerie nodded a thank you to the waitress and when the woman left she slid her cup aside and looked again to Alan.

"Richard and I spent time together off and on," she said. "Our circles didn't exactly overlap, but I think we had something. We weren't going to walk down the aisle anytime soon, but we sometimes held hands."

"You don't seem his type."

"As I said, different circles. I think he liked that." Glancing out the window, she could see the unmarked vehicle parked across the street. She looked back to Alan, indicated his pie. "Eat your pie. You don't want to draw attention."

Alan pulled the plate toward him, then ignored it.

"All right. So you hold hands."

Valerie took a drink from her coffee, lifted a brow at Alan and his untouched slice of pie.

She waited.

Alan picked up his fork, took a bite of the pie.

Only then did she continue.

"Richard and I were at the Gray Swan the night he disappeared," she said. "We left about eleven, went to my place, held hands. That was the last I saw of him; the last anyone saw him, best I can tell."

"His friends?"

"I was the last to see him."

"You went to the police?"

Valerie gave a half-smirk, took another drink of her coffee. She placed the cup carefully back onto the saucer.

"Sure."

She glanced down at the pie. He took another bite, took a swallow of his coffee. She glanced over at the two people seated at the counter, then at the men in the booth at the far end of the café. No one appeared to be paying any mind to her and Alan.

"Listen, if I can help, I'll help. But I've gone down this path. I'm not sure what more we'll find."

"Thanks," Alan said evenly. "So, what's in it for you?"

"Simple justice." That came all too quickly, all too matter-of-factly.

Alan eyed her as if waiting for Valerie to change her answer. She took a thoughtful breath, stared down at her now empty cup.

"Maybe a little revenge," she said.

Alan continued to study her, holding his silence. She gave a shrug then.

"A little money wouldn't hurt."

"Just how do you plan on accomplishing that?"

"No idea. Till you showed up, this whole thing was stuffed in a box."

"Right." He looked away, looked down at the partially eaten pie. He looked up at Valerie. "So what do you think happened?"

"No shortage of ideas on that. Like I said, I've gone down this path. Ideas, not many answers." Valerie wondered aloud then. "William might have something."

"William?"

"A friend," said Valerie. "William kept digging when everyone else gave it up. I can see if he's willing to talk about it."

"I'd appreciate it. You can reach me at Vet Cen 6."

"I know."

At that, Alan looked questioningly at Valerie, and she responded by indicating the ID card on the table. She slid out of the booth.

"Finish your pie," she stated. She left the café.

Alan looked down at the last of his pie as he absently drank the last of his coffee.

Chapter Three

Alan lay asleep in his darkened room, lit only by the dull glow of a neon light coming from outside. A banging on the door brought him awake, though he didn't appear particularly startled. Nor was he surprised or concerned.

He sat up, looked over at the clock on the bedside table. It showed 1:30.

Another bang, bang, bang at the door.

He stood and walked casually to the door, dressed only in undershirt and boxer shorts.

He unlocked and opened the door, again not surprised at what he saw.

Two Willow City police officers stood in the hall. Sgt. Burke was forty years old, tall, strong featured and barrel-chested. His partner was shorter, thinner, younger. Both were wearing well-fitting police uniforms, weapons in holsters.

Burke stepped smoothly through the open doorway, forcing Alan to take a step back into the room. The police sergeant showed a thin, menacing smile, had a sparkle in his eye.

"Good evening, Thornton," he said, looking about the room. "It's been a while."

"Hello, Burke... a few years," said Alan. "I could have gone a few more without seeing your pretty face." He watched Burke's partner come into the room behind Burke, move off to one side and look methodically about.

"Not my call," said Burke. He waved a hand to his partner for him to search the room. He spoke calmly to

Alan as he casually watched his partner toss aside blankets and look through drawers. "What brings you back to our fair city, Thornton?"

"Visiting family."

"I heard about Richard," said Burke. "Tough, that."

His partner turned to Burke and shook his head. Alan raised a brow.

"Were you looking for anything in particular?"

"Not really." Burke gave a final look about the room. "Get dressed. Detective Sullivan would like a word."

At that, Partner reached down and grabbed a pair of pants that were folded on the chair, tossed them to Alan. Alan grabbed them out of the air.

"Sullivan keeps strange hours these days," he said, putting on his pants.

Partner spoke for the first time. "We're none of us happy about it," he said. "We got you to thank for it."

"You know how Sullivan works, Thornton." Burke tapped at his temple. "Always thinking, working the angles." He indicated the door. "Grab your shoes. Let's go."

Alan sat on the edge of the bed and slipped on his shoes, then grabbed his jacket and followed Burke out the door, Partner following.

There was a black sedan parked at the curb in front of the building. Burke guided Alan from the front door across the sidewalk and deposited him into the back seat of the sedan as Partner moved around the vehicle to climb into the driver's seat.

A nondescript man watched from the nearby shadows.

Alan was escorted through the heavy double doors and into the police station lobby. Benches lined the front wall behind them as they entered, currently occupied by several glum-looking customers. Ahead of them was a tall counter with a desk sergeant at his station talking with someone standing before the counter. Beyond the counter, several officers worked at cluttered desks.

Partner moved off as Burke took Alan's arm and guided him across the room toward a wide hallway. He was taken to a small interrogation room and left alone to sit at a metal table to wait for Detective Sullivan. Short curtains were drawn closed in the center of one wall, the familiar interrogation room two-way mirror behind it.

A minute passed. And then another.

The indicator light on the camera that was mounted on the wall turned off as Alan watched.

A minute later, Detective Sullivan entered the room, two folders in hand. He was dressed in a simple suit, his dark hair neatly combed. His expression was calm, unbothered. He looked placidly at Alan as he walked to the table, pulled out the chair opposite Alan and sat down. He set the folders on the table in front of him.

"Hello, Alan," he said. "It's been what, two years?"

Alan slid his arms off the table, sat back and dropped his hands into his lap.

"Detective Sullivan. How's the wife?"

"Which one?" Sullivan spoke as he opened the top folder and began looking through the paperwork.

"Things all right between you and Karen?"

"They are now," said Sullivan. "It's surprising what a divorce can smooth over."

"I'm sorry to hear that."

"Yeah." Sullivan looked over one of the documents in the folder. "Are you enjoying your visit?" He put on a slight smile. "How's Sally's apple pie?"

"Great."

"It is, isn't it? I need to drop in again one of these days. I just never seem to be able to find the time."

"With the hours you keep, I'm not surprised."

"Such is the life of a police officer." Sullivan closed the folder. "You should have come to us, Alan. We'd have been more than happy to provide you with what information we have regarding Richard's disappearance."

"That so?" Alan asked casually.

"All part of the job. We serve the people of Willow City."

"Hey, I'm all ears."

"Yes, well..." Sullivan set aside the top folder, opened the second. He began reading through the documents. "Honestly, there's not much to it. He was brought in for questioning on the evening of June 12, some three months back. He was released several hours later."

"And?"

Sullivan turned the page, glanced over the next sheet. He closed the folder then and set it atop the first.

"He was to be kept under surveillance, but he managed to lose his monitors almost immediately."

"Really..." Alan sounded dubious.

"His whereabouts have been unknown since that evening." He glanced briefly up at Alan, then to the pair of folders. "It is believed that he went into hiding."

Alan studied Sullivan for a long moment. What the detective had said hadn't given him much, but it was information that he could build on. Also, knowing what they were willing to give, and not give, could be valuable.

"Thanks for the info," he said. "Why am I here, Detective?"

Sullivan slowly leaned away from the table, held his hands out in a friendly gesture.

"Just chatting, Alan. Catching up."

"All right. In the spirit of chatting... mind if I ask a question?"

Sullivan said nothing, smiled in answer. Alan took that as a yes.

"Why was Richard brought in for questioning to begin with?" he asked. "He's no criminal. And he has no strong political beliefs one way or the other. He was certainly no threat to Willow City."

Sullivan leaned nearer the table again, indicated the folders that he had set to one side.

"The reason for his interrogation was not specified."

"Really?"

"Curious, I know," said Sullivan. "However, from what I recall of that time, your brother's business interests had grown questionable."

"Richard ran Intercity Trade. Import export. He wasn't even one of the big players. His business was small potatoes; literally."

Sullivan drew a tight smile. "His professional engagements had been broadening."

"Waddya mean, *broadening*?"

"Just what I said."

Alan let that statement lay in the heavy silence for a few moments. What Sullivan was saying may have been true, probably was. It was information Alan would file away for later. But the statement itself... was Sullivan trying to lead Alan toward something, or away from something?

For now, he continued along the line Sullivan was traveling.

"And these *broadened engagements* conflicted with city hall," he stated.

"His discord with others perhaps even more than with us," said Sullivan. He grew thoughtful, silently considered whether to expand on the city-state aspect of that comment. "The bureaucratic dynamics of our city-state haven't changed much since your last visit. Political evolution is a slow process."

"Slow? With one party in permanent control, I'd say it's a dead crawl."

"So you understand. T'wasn't always so, but we work with what we have. Yes?"

Alan said nothing.

Sullivan gave a reflective expression. "I don't believe your brother ever fully got that." He gave an easy nod then. "But you do."

"I do?"

"I can see that. I believe Chief Archer sees it, as well."

Alan pulled on his jacket as he stepped down from the police station front doors and onto the sidewalk. The air had turned cool, the night was dark but for cones of golden light shining down from street-lamp globes.

A vehicle was parked at the curb a hundred yards down the otherwise empty street. Its engine started. It moved slowly forward, stopped in front of Alan. The passenger window opened and Valerie Baker leaned across from the driver's side and looked up at Alan.

"Need a ride?"

Alan opened the passenger door and climbed in. Valerie pulled away from the curb and started up the street.

"So, how ya' doin'?" she asked, a bit heavy on the snarky.

Alan ignored the question. "Doesn't anyone ever sleep in this town? I seem to remember people sleeping."

Valerie, meanwhile, continued along her own thoughts. She glanced briefly at Alan before focusing again on her driving. "One on one with Sullivan?"

"He offered the full support of the Willow City Police Department," he stated flatly.

"Yeah. Quite a guy, that Detective Sullivan."

Alan accepted the sarcasm with a nod, stared out the passenger window, watched the buildings and side streets that passed by.

"Everyone is eager to help," he said. "All this assist, I should have everything wrapped up lickety-split."

"Lickety-split?"

"Sorry. Probably works better if you snap your fingers when you're saying it." He gave an embarrassed shrug. "Kid in my unit used to say it, drove me nuts, but I guess it stuck with me."

They traveled the streets in silence for a time, Alan watching the city passing by. He looked on dispassionately at the sight of several people quickly finishing putting posters up on the side of a building and then hurrying into the shadows.

They turned onto another street. Valerie's expression changed subtly then, the look a bit uncomfortable.

"Sullivan may run his own little fiefdom, but never forget that he works in Archer's shadow, and Police Chief Archer is the mayor's hellhound. They're each on their own power trip, but that power runs uphill, right to city hall."

She looked side-glance at Alan again, noted his blank expression.

"And you, of course, already know all this."

Alan said nothing.

"And you're poking the bear," she realized. "Why are you poking the bear? I'm sure you have a perfectly good reason for doing that."

Alan turned again to the view beyond the passenger window.

"Sometimes the best way to get answers is to listen to their questions," he said.

They reached an intersection and Valerie turned right. She eased the car to the curb in front of the Veterans Center.

Alan looked to Valerie as he opened the door.

"Thanks for the lift." He climbed out of the car, started to close the door, hesitated. He leaned back in, one hand on the roof of the car. "What can you tell me about Richard's business?" he asked.

"He ran Intercity Trade."

"Other than that."

"He kept busy," she said with a shrug. "Beyond that... I couldn't tell you."

"Okay." Alan frowned thoughtfully, finally patted the roof of the car. "Thanks."

"Sure."

He closed the door, watched the car pull away. He looked up and down the street, stuffed his hands into his jacket pockets, turned to the Veterans Center entrance.

The alley was clean. There were several trash cans and a garbage bin lined up neatly along one wall. Doors were set into the brick walls on both sides.

It was pre-dawn, the sun yet to rise above the city. The light that reached into the alley came from a street lamp on the street at the access to the alley.

William Valentine entered the alley, passing under the street lamp. William was middle-aged, middle-height, middle-weight, and a bit disheveled in his clothes and his attention to detail.

He slowed his walk midway down the alley, glanced back once behind him as he continued to a simple door. He pressed a set of numbers on the keypad beside the wall, opened and stepped through the door.

He walked a narrow hallway that was lit by several light fixtures set high on the left wall. There were two security cameras at work. He rounded a corner and started up a steep stairwell. Another camera was set high in one corner at the top of the stairs.

Reaching a tiny landing, he entered another set of numbers on another keypad beside the only door on the landing.

The loft he entered was divided into several areas. To the right was the living area, with couch, chairs and kitchen space; beyond a curtain was a bed and dresser.

To the left was the work area. Computers and monitors were on a long counter beneath a wall of barred windows. Most of the displays were flickering images, video and data. One monitor was displaying the video feeds from the security cameras.

A commercial printer and several smaller printers were lined up along one wall. Stacks of newspapers were piled on tables and chairs, some bundled and bound with twine, some stacked loose.

The loft had the air of constant clutter.

Valerie Baker was sitting on the couch reading a newspaper.

William was of course not surprised at seeing her there.

"Valerie," he said. "Have you been waiting long?"

Valerie set aside the newspaper, indicated a security camera mounted in one corner. "I believe you know exactly how long I've been waiting."

William grinned sheepishly as he moved to the kitchen area. He set about making a pot of coffee.

"I do enjoy the print, William, but it's dangerous. You should stick to your blogs and online news feeds."

William continued making the coffee. "It's all dangerous, Valerie. And I reach a whole different audience with the print."

"Don't give me that," she said. "You print because it bugs the crap out of City Hall."

"There is that." He grew more serious then. "Besides, with the stranglehold they have on tech these days, about the only folks that can read my online feeds are sitting in City Hall."

"Yeah... and they're going to get you one of these days."

"They'll get me in any case; one of these days." He moved to the table and sat facing Valerie. Behind him, the coffee pot was already beginning to burble. "Are you here about Thornton?" he asked.

Chapter Four

Chief Archer entered the Gray Swan and walked toward a booth. At sixty years old, he had a strong, athletic frame, sharp features, and an intense expression. His police uniform was tailored and crisp.

A young police officer followed two paces behind, stood silent nearby as Archer slid into the booth.

The nightclub was empty for Archer, his security man, and the bartender. Eddie drew a mug of beer and brought it over. He set it on the table in front of Archer.

"Good afternoon, Chief. Haven't seen you in here in a while."

Archer picked up the beer and took a swallow. "And yet you remember exactly what I need."

"The secret of a successful bartender, sir," said Eddie. "Never forget a man's favorite poison."

"The stratagem for life, Eddie." Archer took another swallow of his beer. He looked about the empty nightclub. "How's business these days?"

"Good enough to keep the doors open; occasionally a bit more."

"And the show?"

"You know Bonnie and Carl. Never a bad night in the Gray Swan."

"Good to hear," Archer said absently, watched Carl step onto the stage from backstage.

He took another deep draw from his beer.

"Another of these, Eddie. And one of Carl's poison."

"You got it, Chief."

Eddie started back to the bar as Carl came down from the stage and worked his way to Archer's booth. He didn't look particularly pleased to see the police chief, but managed cordiality nonetheless.

"Chief Archer. What brings you to the Gray Swan?"

Archer indicated that Carl should sit; Carl slid in opposite.

"Recent events seemed to warrant an appearance," said Archer.

"Alan Thornton," Carl said matter-of-factly.

Archer's slight grin said yes. "And it offers an opportunity to say hello," he added.

They grew silent when Eddie returned with another beer for Archer and water with lemon for Carl. Archer ignored Eddie, but Carl gave a nod in thank you. Eddie headed back to the bar with the empty mug.

Archer offered Carl a silent salute with his fresh beer, took a swallow.

Carl lifted his water glass but waited to take a drink. "And why would Alan's return home from the war warrant the police chief's visit to our quaint little establishment?"

Archer set his mug carefully down in front him. He watched Carl take a drink of his water and set his glass onto the table.

"I understand Thornton has been dropping in," he said.

"We're a friendly place," said Carl. "He has friends here. And he is living out of the vet center, after all. Where else 'he got to go?"

"Of course." Archer downs the last of his beer, sets the mug down less delicately than before. "And who might these friends be, Carl?"

"Friends. Me. Eddie. Folks."

"Of course. You run a nice club. I've always said so." He glanced casually about the club, back to Carl. "How's your sister these days? Her voice holding up?"

"Bonnie is fine, thanks. Quite well, actually."

"Good to hear. Maybe I'll drop in later, catch a set."

"Any time. We'll be here."

"Good, good." Archer slid out of the booth. He looked down at Carl. "And Carl... next time you see Alan, you be sure tell him I said hello."

"I'll do that," Carl said coolly.

The security officer stepped to one side as Archer started to the door, then followed after him two paces behind.

Carl took a drink from his water, stared thoughtfully at the glass. Eddie came over to the booth while looking questioningly in the direction of the closing front door.

"Carl? What the hell was that all about?"

"I can't say for sure, Eddie. But if I had to guess, I'd have to say it was a warning." He lifted his glass. *"Watch your step... they be watching."*

The "Truth in Reporting" news broadcast was displaying on the television monitor in the Veterans Center lounge, the newscaster sitting at her anchor desk. The screen behind her was displaying an image of the broad avenue in front of the Federal Capital building.

Alan and an elderly veteran were sitting in a pair of easy chairs in the lounge, watching the broadcast.

"Welcome back to the afternoon edition of Truth in Reporting, a service of the National Education Office." read the news anchor. "We take you now to the Federal Capital, where excitement is building for this year's Founding Day and Ball."

The monitor display expanded to focus on the image behind the newscaster, filling the screen, changing then from a static image to a video showing workers putting together bleachers, barriers, canopies. The elderly veteran sitting next to Alan grumbled and shook his head sorrowfully, his attention focused on the story.

"Veterans find work," said the old vet, somber sarcasm.

"Excuse me?" asked Alan.

The old vet nodded at the monitor displaying the workers in action.

"Two weeks work. A week putting it all together, a week taking it all down." He gave a side-glance to Alan. "Oh, joy."

Cavanaugh came into the lounge then, dropped into a chair near Alan. He glanced once at the monitor, quickly dismissed the story and looked at Alan.

"Thornton. Do you know you already have this town abuzz?" he asked.

"I haven't done anything yet," said Alan, while pointedly continuing to watch the monitor.

"You're too modest. Your very presence is shining a light on what most around here would prefer remain in the shadows."

"Oh, you're just saying that."

The exchange was bringing a curious gaze from the elderly veteran. The news story on the television monitor continued, now little more than background noise.

Cavanaugh shifted nearer Alan. "Mr. Cain would like to meet with you," he said.

"To offer his help?" Alan's kept his eyes on the monitor.

Cavanaugh grinned. "In person."

The Truth in Reporting broadcast returned to the studio and the woman at the anchor desk.

The large, black sedan pulled up to the curb in front of Cain's Club. The front passenger door opened and Cavanaugh stepped out. A moment later the rear passenger door opened and Alan stepped out onto the wide, clean sidewalk.

The building before them was two-storey, with small windows spanning the second floor on either side of a colorful sign reading "Cain's Club" above the glass front door.

Cavanaugh walked to the front door and opened it, moved aside and gestured for Alan to enter.

A security guard in the foyer stood silent in Alan's path. Alan lifted his arms and held them out. The guard patted him down and then moved aside, nodded crisply to Cavanaugh as Cavanaugh escorted Alan the rest of the way into the club.

Arthur Cain was sitting at a table near the back of the club, was focused now on two ledgers that were on the table in front of him. An associate dressed in suit and tie stood nearby.

Cain was in his sixties, had a large frame, was neat and well-groomed. He glanced briefly up at the approaching Alan and Cavanaugh, closed one ledger, returned his attention to the open pages of the second.

Alan and Cavanaugh stopped several short paces from table and waited. Cain closed the second ledger, gathered the two books together and handed them the waiting associate. He nodded dismissal and the associate departed with the ledgers.

Cain focused his attention then on Alan.

"Mr. Thornton. Good of you to come."

"Happy to oblige, Mr. Cain." Alan's tone was flat.

Cain gave Cavanaugh a dismissive nod. Cavanaugh nodded in answer, took a step back, turned about and left. Cain indicated that Alan take the chair opposite, then waited for him to sit down.

"I understand you are home for good, Mr. Thornton."

"Can't say that's definite," said Alan. "Not yet."

"You're retired, I hear."

"That's right."

"Messy thing, the war." Cain appeared to grow thoughtful. "I never fully understood it, myself."

"Yeah, well... done with it, now."

"Home safe, then."

Alan gave a knowing half-smile at that comment, held his silence. Seeing Alan's smirk, Cain chuckled lightly in understanding.

"Yes, I suppose safety is a relative concept, isn't it?"

Alan held his slight smile, held his silence. After a few moments, Cain continued.

"You are looking into your brother's disappearance," he stated.

"I am," said Alan. This time it was Cain who held his silence, and so Alan went on. "Is this something you might be able to help me with?"

"I could make a few inquiries," said Cain.

"Nothing you can pass along right now, then..."

"Nothing beyond what you no doubt already know. Our city-state's uniformed finest picked him up; that was that."

"Any idea what my brother might have gotten himself into that would have attracted the wrong sort of attention?"

Cain considered, wore a shrewd smile. "Richard ran a trade business, so I understand."

"That doesn't quite answer my question though, does it?"

Cain looked to one side, raised a hand. His associate appeared as if out of nowhere. Cain looked back to Alan.

"Thirsty?" he asked.

"I'm fine," said Alan. "Thanks."

Cain spoke to his associate. "A water, please."

The associate left to get his water and Cain looked back to Alan.

"Richard had been pursuing certain gray market activities for several months prior to his disappearance," he said. "I believe the mayor suggested that he find another hobby."

"Gray market... outside his trade business."

"So I understand," said Cain.

"Like what? The man was trading vegetables, textiles."

Cain's associate returned with his glass of water. Cain waited while he set the glass on the table and again stepped back into the shadows.

"I have been told that his interests had expanded beyond acceptable boundaries," he stated then. "Who's to say why? Who's to say where such a path might lead?"

"Expanded to what?"

Cain only shrugged in answer, calmly took a drink of his water.

Alan frowned. "I would think such a path undertaken by my brother would be something you would be interested in; one way or another."

"When his activities drew the attention of City Hall, I began monitoring the situation. His subsequent disappearance precluded pursuing it further."

"I can't imagine you would let something like that go so easily," said Alan.

"Let it go?" Cain slowly shook his head. "Why do you think you are here?"

"You are monitoring the situation." Alan's statement was a flat comment.

Cain gave a placid, considered smile in response. They were silent for several long moments.

"What's going on, Cain?" Alan asked at last. "Where's my brother?"

"I honestly don't know," said Cain. "If I did, I wouldn't need you."

Alan said nothing to that. Cain continued.

"As you noted, the path Richard chose was of some interest to me."

"And I am here because...?"

"I am touching base with an old friend."

Cavanaugh reappeared, apparently in response to some unseen signal from Cain. He stood several paces from the table and waited. Cain ignored him for the moment, continued his conversation with Alan.

"I have enjoyed our visit, Mr. Thornton. It really takes me back." He took another drink of his water, set the glass down in front of him. "We shall do this again."

Alan slowly slid his chair back and stood up. "I look forward to hearing the results of your enquiries."

"Of course, Mr. Thornton." Cain gave a curt nod in Cavanaugh's direction. "Mr. Cavanaugh will see you home."

Alan was dismissed. He followed Cavanaugh toward the front of the club. Cain didn't give him a glance. He looked across to the bar, subtly raised a hand and lowered it.

The bartender began preparing a drink.

Alan sat at the small desk in his room, was looking over an old-style revolver. Turning the spindle, he could see there were three cartridges.

Chavez leaned against the wall beside the desk. He folded his arms across his chest.

"I put out a few feelers, asked a few questions," he said, watching Alan. "Not much new, I'm afraid. The connections just aren't there anymore."

"I understand," said Alan, reseating the spindle. He turned the spindle to an empty cylinder against the hammer.

"Word is, though... you're making some folks nervous," said Chavez. "Folks who were happy to see the Richard Thornton disappearance fade away."

"I've been hearing the same thing." Alan indicated the weapon. "This is in no way traceable back to you?"

"Clean as they come, my friend." He watched Alan opened a desk drawer and placed the weapon in the drawer. "What do you plan on doing with it?"

Alan closed the drawer, leaned back in his chair. "Nothing. I hope."

William walked across the room and opened the front door. He welcomed Valerie and Alan into his loft with a gesture.

"Good afternoon, Valerie." He gave a nod then to Alan. "Mr. Thornton. Welcome." He closed the door behind them and followed them back into the room.

"Nice place," said Alan.

"I like it." William started toward the table, urged them to sit and then went to the kitchenette counter. "Coffee?" he asked.

"Water, thanks," said Alan.

"Nothing for me, William," said Valerie, sitting opposite Alan. "Thank you."

William brought a glass down from the cupboard and filled it at the sink, spoke then as he brought it to Alan. "Thornton, Alan. Master Sergeant." He quickly raised a finger. "Retired."

Alan indicated the empty chair, waited for William to sit down.

"William Valentine," he said then. "Newspaper man, investigative reporter. Trouble-stirrer extraordinaire."

"I do nothing more than take information that I find and put it into words."

Alan looked side-glance to Valerie, then pointedly to William.

"The talent is to know where to find that information, and then to understand what it is you are seeing."

William accepted the complement, leaned back in his chair.

"You're looking for information on your brother's disappearance."

"That's right," said Alan. "What can you tell me?"

"A bit, though probably no more than what you already know."

"I know that he was pulled in for questioning, that he disappeared sometime after that."

"Your brother had been butting heads with City Hall for some time leading up to that night," said William. "It was inevitable."

"He had been involved in the gray market," stated Alan.

"So I understand."

"What specifically, in this gray market?"

"To get him disappeared? More than your everyday contraband. Everyday smuggling shouldn't get you gone." He gave a slow shake of the head. "You're brother wasn't political. His activities may have been criminal, but not political. So... I figure there's something else."

Valerie entered the conversation with an observation.

"He seldom talked politics," she said. To William then, dubious, "William?"

"He wasn't trying to bring down City Hall, but he always seemed to be at odds with 'em; them, and with Cain."

Alan shook his head and frowned. "Cain doesn't know where he is. I'm fairly sure of that."

"You are probably correct. I do think, however, that he knows something of how he disappeared."

"You do..."

William set his hand with his thumb out as if readying to count points. Beginning with point one... "Richard

Thornton was released from custody following interrogation. That we know."

"And they had him followed," agreed Alan.

One of William's fingers joined his raised thumb in counting points. Point two... "And they lost him. I don't think he accomplished that on his own."

"You think Cain snatched him," said Alan, a statement more than a question.

Another finger up. Point three... "Or tried to."

"Like I said, I'm pretty sure Cain doesn't know where Richard is."

"And I agree."

"So?"

William slowly closed his hand, brought it down. He shrugged.

"That was as far as I my investigation took me. He gave them the slip when they first tried to snatch him up, or he got away from them later, or they let him walk and he ditched 'em..." he looked hesitantly to Valerie. "I don't know."

The three were silent then.

William indicated Alan's glass of water, as yet untouched.

"I have lemon," he said. "Would you like lemon with that?"

Several hours later, William stood at the sink washing a dinner plate as classic jazz played quietly in the background. Evening gray showed through the wall of windows.

The music stopped.

An alert beeped softly and then stopped.

William turned about and looked across the loft in the direction of the security monitor. He stepped around the table and moved nearer the monitor.

The display showed three police officers walking up the alley. They stopped at William's alley door. One of the officers pulled the cover plate from the keypad beside the door and another attached two wires from a small electronic device he was holding to thc internals of the keypad.

William moved away from the security monitor and over to the bookshelf. He reached into the shelf, released a catch to a hollow click sound. He pulled the shelf wall open, revealing a hidden closet behind. He stepped into the closet and pulled the shelf closed to the sound of the hollow click.

The security monitor displayed the police officers working their way up the narrow stairwell to the landing.

From inside the closet, William heard the front door opening. He heard the rustling of the officers moving about in the loft. There came the sound of furniture being tossed aside, computer equipment being tossed to the floor.

It grew quiet then...

Out in the loft, one office stood stoically at the wall of windows, was looking out at the evening. A second officer stood amidst computers, monitors and printers that were now scattered about the floor. He was holding one of William's recent newspapers, was casually reading to himself.

The third officer was in the kitchen area, was holding the dinner plate in hand. It was still warm from recently having been washed. He looked back into the center of the room. He casually tossed the plate aside. It crashed to the floor.

In the hidden closet, William nervously closed his eyes to the sound of the officers again shuffling about in the loft. After another minute, there came the sound of the front door closing.

He waited a few moments more, then lifted a hand and pushed a button in the wall beside him. A small monitor inset in the wall came to life, the light of the monitor shining on his face.

The display showed the three officers descending the stairs.

In the loft, another half-minute passed. There was a hollow click sound, and the shelf wall opened. William stepped cautiously out of hiding.

He moved into the middle of the room and took in the midst of the destruction all about the loft.

Chapter Five

The Gray Swan was two-thirds full. Carl and Bonnie were up on the stage, Carl at the piano, Bonnie at the microphone. They were nearing the end of a song heavy on nightclub blues. Chief Archer was sitting in one of the booths, Alan and Valerie in the next booth over.

Valerie looked past Alan in the direction of the police chief. She leaned across the table and said something to Alan. When Alan turned and looked back over his shoulder, Archer lifted his beer in a silent hello, his expression giving away nothing. Alan gave an acknowledging nod in return, turned about again and faced forward.

Up on the stage, Bonnie finished her song. Alan and the others in the audience clapped politely.

"Thank you, everyone," said Bonnie. "We're going to take a short break, but we'll be back with another set in a few minutes. So don't you go anywhere."

She looked briefly to Alan; her smile faded when she saw Archer in the booth beyond. She took the few steps over to Carl and leaned on her brother's piano. She took a drink from a glass tumbler, took a lit cigarette from Carl and drew on it, handed it back. She turned again to look out across crowd.

Below in the audience, Alan and Valerie were in quiet conversation.

"Just what is it you do, Miss Baker?" asked Alan.

"It's *Miss Baker*, now?"

"Valerie," conceded Alan.

Valerie accepted that, sighed thoughtfully. "Oh, a little of this, some of that. You know."

"Interesting line of work, that. Does it pay well?"

"It keeps me off the street," she said.

"Good to hear." Alan took a drink from his iced tea, set the glass down with more care than was necessary. "This work... is that how you met William?"

"William and I have been friends a long time. You might say his work and mine occasionally coincide."

"Is that so? That's revealing in a shadowy sort of way," said Alan. "And Carl?"

"What about Carl?"

"How does his work and yours coincide?"

"Why do you ask?"

"Just curious. He works a nightclub, and yet he sends me to you. Have you been friends a long time as well?"

"Our paths cross now and again," she said, keeping her slight smile.

Alan studied Valerie for a few moments, absently took another drink.

"I've known Carl and Bonnie a while, myself," he said. "Strange that your path and mine have never crossed."

"Is it?"

"It is."

They grew silent then. Alan looked again over his shoulder to Archer. He turned back to Valerie, pushed his glass aside.

"On the subject of crossed paths... back in a sec," he said. He slid out of the booth and worked his way to Archer. He gave a quick glance to security, a friendly smile to Archer.

"Evening, Chief. Mind if I sit down?"

Archer indicated the bench opposite and Alan slid into the booth.

"Dropped in for the show?" he asked.

Archer clasped his beer with both hands, indicated the stage.

"I just had to catch a song," he said. "She's quite the lady."

"You dropped in to catch a song?"

"What other reason could there be?"

"I can't imagine," said Alan.

"And you?" asked Archer, though more of a statement than a question. "Are you just here for the show?"

"I like the company."

"Of course. I believe I heard as much."

"Is that so..."

"It is." Archer took another long swallow of his beer. He set the mug down and looked absently at it as he spoke. "Will you be in town long?"

"I haven't decided. It could go either way."

Archer smiled knowingly at that. "I can appreciate that. A lot of factors come into play, do they not?"

"Two or three."

"You let me know if we can help with any of them; glad to help, you being an awarded veteran and all." Archer looked past Alan to the stage then, where Bonnie appeared to be preparing for the next set.

"Ah. Here we go," he said. "The lady sings."

The conversation appeared to be at an end. Alan studied Archer a second more, then slid out of the booth. He made brief eye contact with Bonnie, up on the stage, as stepped back to his own booth. There was a hint of concern in her expression.

He slid in opposite Valerie.

"And?" she asked.

"Apparently City Hall is eager to help returning veterans."

Valerie looked over Alan's shoulder to Archer. He was focused on Bonnie.

Bonnie began another bluesy jazz song.

City Hall was a solid, imposing structure. Steep steps rose from the wide sidewalk street-side up to four concrete pillars fronting the building through which a set of double doors was visible. A security officer stood at either end of the pillar landing.

A long black sedan pulled up to the curb. The front passenger door opened and Archer's personal security man got out. He moved smoothly to the back door and opened it.

Chief Archer climbed out of the sedan. He took a moment to let the morning sun warm his face, gave an absent nod to his security before walking across the sidewalk and climbing the steps, his security several paces behind.

Another pair of well-armed security guards stood beside the doors. They said nothing as Archer passed through.

A security officer stood beside the check-in station in the center of the main foyer, a large, hollow main hall. Archer ignored the station and the guard, walked past and on to the wide staircase beyond, leaving his personal security to move to one side of foyer, stand with his back to the wall and wait.

Archer took the stairs to the second floor. He entered the mayor's office reception area; the mayor's personal secretary sat at her desk, prim and proper and dedicated to her duties. The chief passed a small waiting area on the left and continued ahead and around the reception desk on his way toward the large, heavy wooden door beyond. A brass plate on door read "Mayor".

The receptionist looked up from her work.

"Chief Archer. The Mayor is expecting you."

"Thank you, Betty."

The Mayor glanced across his desk as Archer entered the office, but he otherwise ignored his police chief. He was leaning back in his leather chair, in casual conversation on the phone.

The Mayor was in his sixties, was graying at the temples, his straight hair combed neatly back. His attire was professional but casual. He appeared strong and healthy. His voice was clear and confident.

The office consisted of fine wood, curtain-trimmed windows, leather furniture. Fine paintings hung on the walls. A television monitor was mounted on one wall, at the moment turned off.

The Mayor sat behind a large, heavy desk. On the desk was a flat-screen computer monitor and keyboard, a stack of several folders, and a small figurine of a dragon.

Archer took another step nearer the desk, then to one side. He stood silent, waited patiently.

The Mayor was talking on the phone to the president.

"No sir. No sir. I understand," he said, then listened for several moments. "Absolutely, Mr. President. You're absolutely right, sir."

The Mayor shifted about and faced forward, leaned forward and placed one forearm on the desk.

"Of course, Mr. President," he went on. "Count on it. Absolutely. No, no, I certainly will."

There was a long pause as the Mayor listened. There appeared to be a shift in the one-sided conversation. The Mayor smiled then.

"Yes sir. Yes sir. Jenny is looking forward to it. We both are. I'll see you then, Mr. President." There was another moment's pause. The Mayor gave another smile. "Yes sir. I will, sir."

The Mayor let out a long sigh as he hung up the phone. His smile vanished as he looked darkly across at Chief Archer.

"Federation Founding Ball next week," he said.

"Yes, Mr. Mayor," said Archer.

"I hate the Founding Ball."

"I understand, sir."

"The music is annoying. And I don't dance. I don't like dancing."

Archer let the comment go, waited for what he expected to be coming.

The Mayor breathed noisily, frowned and shifted his shoulders.

"The president has concerns. The president has no problem expressing those concerns."

"Sir?"

"It is imperative that whatever issues we have in own little city-state stay within the borders of our own little city-state."

Archer said nothing, waited for the Mayor to continue. The Mayor stared down at his hands, leaned back then in his chair. He spoke without looking up at Archer.

"Eight autonomous city-states in the Federation, and Willow City dominates the President's daily brief more often than not; one thing and another." He hesitated, frowned darkly, looked up at Archer. "I'll not have Federation boots on our streets, Archer."

There was a long moment of uncomfortable silence between the two men. Varied thoughts appeared then to cross the Mayor's face as shadows.

"What's all this nonsense about Richard Thornton's brother?" he asked.

"Alan Thornton is not a problem, Mr. Mayor."

"Why is he still breathing?"

"Sir..." said Archer. "I'd like to keep our options open. We might be able to use him. He might be able to open doors that we cannot."

The Mayor looked piercingly across the desk to Archer.

"To find his brother?" he asked. "Do you really think Thornton is still alive?"

"I've never thought otherwise."

The mayor thought through his next words very carefully, spoke his next words very precisely.

"If he is alive, then get him. I want this done once and for all. I want that network. Then throw him in the river, his brother after him."

Alan stepped out the front door of the Veterans Center, paused to take in the early evening. He frowned when he saw Sgt. Burke's partner leaning against a car parked at the curb, his arms folded, watching him.

Alan walked toward the car, noting Sgt. Burke sitting in the front passenger seat, the window rolled down.

"Burke," said Alan. "Out for an evening drive?"

Burke looked sidelong up at Alan.

"Detective Sullivan asked that I pass along a message."
Burke's words were dry. "He managed to squeeze that visit
to Sally's into his busy schedule."

"Good to hear. Those little moments are important."

"Right," said Burke. He rubbed the bridge of his nose.
"There is an invitation attached."

"Ah…" Alan straightened, looked up and down the street.
"I'm finding myself in a number of these chats lately."

Burke wasn't thrilled at playing Sullivan's messenger
boy. "Uh, huh. I expect you're downright popular."

Partner opened the rear passenger door and waited. His
expression was cool, his eyes cold.

"Thank you, my man," said Alan, climbing in.

Burke looked absently outward as Partner climbed in
behind the wheel and started the car.

Alan came into the café, calmly took in the scene. A few
people sat at the counter, several of the booths were
occupied. Detective Sullivan was sitting alone in one of the
middle booths and looked to be working on a slice of apple
pie.

Sgt. Burke gave Alan a light shove from behind, pushing
him away from the door so that he and his partner could
get around him and head to the counter. Alan walked down
the row of booths, slid in opposite Sullivan.

The detective set his fork next to the plate, picked up his
coffee cup and took a sip. He set the cup down onto the
saucer. He picked up his fork and took another bite.

"Second slice," he said. "Best pie in town."

"I'm surprised you were able to make the time."

"Simple matter of priorities, Mr. Thornton." Sullivan took
another forkful of pie. "Speaking of which, how's your
investigation going?"

"Only just starting," said Alan.

The waitress made an appearance with a coffee mug and
carafe. She filled the cup and set it front of Alan, then
refilled Sullivan's.

Sullivan pointed to his pie and then to Alan, gave a wink to the waitress.

"A slice for my friend here," he said.

"Coming up." The waitress left to get Alan's pie.

Sullivan took a sip of from his refilled cup. "I understand you dropped in to see Cain."

"I accepted his invitation."

"Right. I've had a few of those myself over the years. Turning it down could prove awkward."

"The man offered his help."

Sullivan took the last bite of his pie. His set his fork onto the empty plate.

"Did he?"

"I've gotten a few such offers."

Sullivan grinned at that. "I'll bet."

The waitress returned with a slice of pie for Alan.

"Thank you, my dear," said Sullivan.

"Yes, thank you," said Alan.

"You're welcome." The waitress looked from Alan to Sullivan, then left.

Another grin from Sullivan.

"I get a discount," he said.

Alan took a forkful of pie. Sullivan watched.

"Good, huh?" he asked.

Alan poked and prodded at his serving of pie.

"Listen, Detective," he said. "The pie's great, the coffee's great, and I don't want to sound unappreciative... but why am I here?"

Sullivan glanced casually about the café... in the direction of the waitress behind the counter, at Burke and Partner at the end of the counter. He took another swallow of his coffee, looked again at Alan.

"We've known each other a long time, Alan. Now and again, we've even been friends. Of a sort."

"All right," said Alan. "I'll give you that."

"Good. So, given that, we may not be double dating these days, but you need to know we're not on opposite sides."

Alan considered, finally lifted a fork of apple pie. "Hey, we're sharing Sally's finest."

"A positive sign, at that," said Sullivan. "With that in mind, I want you to think hard on what I say."

Alan gave a slow nod.

"All right," he said. "You have my attention."

Sullivan pushed aside his empty pie plate and leaned nearer Alan while trying not to appear conspiratorial.

"I'm not asking you to stop searching—"

"Good call."

"Yeah, well, no one expects you to just walk away from this. It is for that very reason that interested parties have decided to wait and watch."

"Oh, I got that," said Alan.

"Good. And when you start getting answers?"

Sullivan watched Alan for a sign that he understood. Meanwhile, Alan waited for more, but nothing came.

"Right," said Alan. "I get it."

Sullivan accepted that. He leaned back, bringing his cup with him. He took a deep swallow of coffee, stared at the cup, looked then about the café.

"Alan..." he said quietly. "I'm not Archer."

"I'd hate to think there'd be two of him."

Sullivan didn't appear amused. He stared wearily at Alan. Alan shrugged, wore a slightly apologetic look.

"Now and again, you're not so bad."

"Right," Sullivan sighed tiredly. He slid out of the booth, looked down at Alan. "Step carefully, Master Sergeant."

He looked over at Sgt. Burke and Partner, sitting at the counter. When Burke looked his way, Sullivan gave a nod and started toward the door.

Burke and Partner slid off their stools and followed as Sullivan left the café.

Chapter Six

The cab pulled away from the curb and continued down the street, leaving Alan standing before the warehouse. There was one door set into the otherwise featureless wall; a small sign above the door read "Intercity Trade Co.".

The Intercity Trade warehouse was one of a number of nondescript one- and two-storey warehouse structures set along the wide, low-traffic street that ran down the heart of the east district. Alan walked past the door and on to the corner of the building, then to an open gate that was set into a tall cyclone-mesh fence. There were several loading bay doors along this side of the building, two box trailers parked in a far corner of the enclosed lot.

Alan took a set of wooden steps up to an unmarked door and went inside. He walked across the small lobby and stepped around the counter. There was no one at the only desk. Windows set into the wall on Alan's right revealed the open warehouse floor. He could see half a dozen collections of assorted boxes and crates, but the floor was otherwise empty.

He continued into a narrow back hallway. He looked through the first open door into an office that appeared to have recently been in use. Lights were turned on, the computer monitor was active. The small plaque on the open door read "John Benton".

No one was in the office.

Alan continued to the next office door. This one was closed. The door plaque read "Richard Thornton." He opened the door and went into the office; it was simple, sparse. Bookshelves covered the wall on the left. A plain desk and chair was in the middle of the room, a guest chair to Alan's right.

He didn't know what he was looking for, didn't know if he would recognize it if he saw it. He wandered over to the shelves, glanced at the titles of several books. He picked up and looked through a stack of folders.

He sensed something then, looked in the direction of the door.

John Benton stood in the open doorway, his shoulder resting against the jamb, arms folded.

Benton was thirty years old, clean-cut, dressed in casual button shirt and slacks.

"I expected you long before now, Alan," he said.

"Hey, John." Alan set the folders back on the shelf, started over to the desk. "Distractions. You know..."

"So I hear."

Alan sat at Richard's desk, leaned back in the chair. He looked about the office, then to Benton, who was still standing in the doorway.

"Business in a slump?" he asked.

"City hall pulled our license," said Benton. "They confiscated what they wanted, left me to sell off what's left in inventory."

"How'd they do that? Pull your license?"

"Tagged Richard with illegal activities."

"Right. Sorry, man," said Alan. He began looking through the desk drawers. "What was he up to?"

"I don't know. Honest." Benton pushed off the door jamb and took a step into the room. He nodded in the direction of his own office next door. "My office was mostly for show. I didn't really do much around here. Assistant's assistant at best. Our secretary had more status, and she was part time."

Alan didn't respond, continued looking through the desk.

"Honest," said Benton.

"Oh, I believe you. Richard is a one man show from way back." Alan lifted a box from the large bottom drawer and set it on the desk. "So, what are your plans now, Mr. Benton?"

"I'm taking my time shuttering up the place." A weak smile then. "You never know."

"Sure," Alan said absently. He looked through assorted items in the metal box, brought out a key card. "Is Richard's apartment still over on Ashland?"

The apartment complex consisted of six single-storey fourplex buildings nestled into garden-like grounds. Alan walked the grounds to the building with Richard's apartment, heard a voice call out to him as he approached the door.

"Hey, sweetie. Long time, no see."

He turned to see Wanda coming towards him, following the winding walkway across the grounds. She was about forty years old, tall, slim, her hair in a beehive hairdo, wrinkles at the corners of her eyes behind frame glasses. She wore casual slacks and blouse.

"Hello, Wanda."

Wanda stopped a short pace from Alan. She folded her arms across her chest and gave a smile.

"I heard you were back in town," she said.

"Must've been a flyer put out," said Alan.

Her smile broadened, and there was something behind it. "You always were one to keep things interesting, sweetie." Her smile faded. "You holdin' up okay? Ya' know, your brother and all?"

"I'll be fine."

"Of course you will." She gave a nod to the apartment. "He's gone, ya' know. Tough to say, tougher to hear, but..."

"Might be so."

"City won't let me put the apartment on the market. And no compensation, to boot."

"I'm sure they'll let it go before too long, Wanda. The facts will come out, soon enough."

"Hope that's so," said Wanda. She considered for a moment, studied Alan. "I heard you were retiring, Alan. Ya' home for good?"

"Might be. A few things to sort out before I can say for sure."

Wanda gave another nod to the apartment. "Ya' interested?" she asked. "You'll be needin' a place."

"Might be. Let's see how things play out." He raised the key card and indicated that he was going into the apartment.

"Yes, Sure. Of course." she started away, stopped and looked back. She gave a smile and a wink. "Love to have you as a neighbor, sweetie. Just say the word."

She turned away again, disappeared around the corner of the building. Alan turned back to the front door of the apartment.

The main room of the apartment was divided into living and kitchen areas, separated by an island counter. The living area had a couch and chair, coffee and side tables, a television monitor on the wall. The kitchen area beyond the counter was dully lit, sunlight streaming hazily through a pair of windows in the far wall.

Much of the apartment was in disarray; furniture pushed askew, drawers open and items strewn on the floor. It appeared the apartment had been searched.

Alan conducted a quick cursory search of his own, looking into several open drawers and the front closet. He squatted down beside assorted mail that had been strewn on the floor, reading the envelopes and tossing them back to the floor.

He moved into the kitchen, opened and looked in the cupboards. Opening the refrigerator, he found a number of jars, a few sealed plastic containers, and two plates with leftovers long ago gone bad.

He stepped back into the living area and on into the hallway. He looked briefly into the one bedroom, then the bathroom. He returned then to the living room.

He stood unmoving for several moments, then went to the front door. He reached out and turned the lock as he looked back into the living room. Safe then, he went into the kitchen and found a butter knife in the utensils drawer. In the living room, he pulled the couch away from the wall. Kneeling down at the wall, he used the knife to free a section of the baseboard. This exposed an opening in the wall two inches tall, twelve inches wide.

He pulled a small box from the hidden compartment.

Whatcha got here, Richard?

Opening the box, he found small ink cartridges lined up side by side. He lifted one out, looked curiously at it. It was a cartridge for an inkjet printer.

What the... Alan wrinkled his brow.

Why had Richard hidden half a dozen ink cartridges in his secret wall compartment?

He turned the cartridge about in his hand several times, frowned, put it back with the others. He closed the box and returned it to its hiding place.

Valerie was sitting alone in her usual booth in Sally's Café, both hands absently wrapped about a cup of coffee. It was evening, and the city beyond the wall of windows was gray, the evenly spaced street lamps creating misty globes of light in the thin fog.

Several of the other booths were occupied, as were a handful of the stools at the counter. The waitress stood behind the counter, her arms crossed, looking a bit bored.

Carl came into the café. He looked about, took in the scene, and then walked over to Valerie's booth.

"Good evening, Valerie," he said, sliding into the booth opposite.

"Carl." Valerie took a sip from her coffee, set the cup carefully onto the saucer. "How are things at the Gray Swan?"

"Same as always. Getting by."

The waitress came over to the booth, stood silent. Carl glanced up at her.

"Nothing, thanks," he said.

The waitress looked coolly down at Carl, made no sign to leave. Carl sighed, pulled out his ID card and held it out for her.

"Coffee," he stated.

"On me," said Valerie.

Carl smoothly withdrew his card before the waitress had a chance to take it.

"Thanks," he said.

They waited then until the waitress left and they were again alone.

"The loft was trashed," said Valerie. Her voice was low but not an obvious whisper. "No sign of William."

"They get him?"

"I don't think so. We'd have heard something."

Carl took a moment to think that through. "He's gone dark then," he said at last.

The waitress returned with a coffee carafe and cup. She filled the cup and set it before Carl, then refilled Valerie's. Valerie held her ID card up by two fingers. The waitress took the card and stepped away from the booth.

"D'you hear anything from the Alliance?" asked Carl.

"They're not talking."

"But you think they know something."

"They're Alliance," said Valerie. "Of course they know something."

"Are they hiding him?"

"Maybe. At the very least, protecting him."

Carl frowned, hesitated, finally took a drink from his coffee. "William is one of theirs," he said.

"Some rather close ties," said Valerie, shrugging. She leaned nearer. "He's my friend."

"They know that." Carl leaned back. He and Valerie looked thoughtfully at one another for several moments. Muted voices came from other booths.

"They've pulled back," he said. "Not likely to open up to anyone not fully Alliance."

"Oh, you've noticed that, eh?" Valerie stared down at her cup. "No one wants to talk. No one wants to be seen with folks like us. And business... gone to ground."

"I don't see that changing until Alan finds Richard."

Valerie gave a half nod, considered.

"Everybody has something to hide. Everybody has something to protect."

"Everybody wants something," said Carl.

"Including me." Valerie lifted her cup, looked over the rim at Carl. "Including you."

Alan's face was faintly aglow from the neon light shining in through the window into his room. He was relaxing on his bed atop the covers, his feet up, legs crossed at his ankles; his shoes were off but was still otherwise dressed. He was watching a news broadcast that was displaying on his television monitor.

The broadcast image was of the mayor and his wife walking to a limousine, his security ever present. The newscaster noted that the mayor and his wife would soon be departing for the Federation Capitol, where they would be attending the Founding Ball.

The Mayor was looking forward to it.

Alan appeared bored, stared dully at the flickering monitor.

Chapter Seven

Midmorning in the Gray Swan; the lights were on. Eddie was sweeping the floor; a teenager was bussing a booth.

Carl and Alan were sitting at the bar facing one another, water glasses on the counter beside them. The nightclub was otherwise empty.

"So, how do you know Valerie?" asked Alan. "What's the connection with Richard?"

"Valerie and Richard had a thing," said Carl, almost matter-of-factly.

"I get that. They held hands. It's more than that."

Carl sighed softly, lifted his glass of water, set it back on the counter.

"Valerie and I..." he started, "had a shared concern that Richard was getting involved in something that was going to get him into trouble."

"You were concerned for Richard's wellbeing, Valerie was concerned for his wellbeing, and that brought the two of you together?"

"Something like that."

"I see." Alan took a drink of his water. He looked about the room, ensured that the kid cleaning the tables was out of earshot. "And how did this involve ink cartridges?"

"Ink cartridges?"

"Ink cartridges. For printers."

Carl shook his head, looked away from Alan.

"Richard had been getting deeper into the gray market," he said. "I suppose that could include ink cartridges."

"Ink? Really?"

"Ink is controlled. So is paper."

Carl was looking across at the wall behind the bar, making it hard for Alan to read his expression.

The man was hiding something...

"Ink cartridges, worth a disappear?" he asked.

"I guess that would depend on the market," shrugged Carl.

"And what would that market be?"

"I couldn't tell ya." Carl turned about on the stool and stood up. "Sorry, man. Things to do. See ya' later?"

"Yeah. Sure. Later." Alan faced forward, took a drink from his water as Carl walked toward the back of the club.

Eddie worked his way along the bar until he was standing opposite Alan.

"Refill?"

Alan stared down at his glass, swallowed the last of his water. He set the glass on the bar.

"One's my limit," he said, slid off the stool. "Later, Eddie."

Leaving the club, he walked out to the curb. The street was quiet; no people, no cars, this despite it being the middle of the day.

He stuffed his hands into his jacket and started up the street.

An unmarked police car appeared then, coming up the street from behind Alan. It traveled slowly. There was a simple flashing light magnetically attached to the roof just above the front passenger window.

A prisoner van was following directly behind the sedan.

The two vehicles passed Alan and continued up the street. They crossed the intersection ahead, continued on and turned at the next intersection.

The street was again silent and still but for Alan.

Alan came in through the front door and started across the lobby of the Veterans Center. Several veterans were relaxing in the lounge for the evening, the monitor displaying the mayor and wife arriving in the Federation Capitol.

The desk clerk stepped up to the counter as Alan neared the front desk on his way to the stairs.

"Master Sergeant Thornton," he called out, holding a small envelope. "A message for you."

"Thank you." Alan took the envelope, opened at it as he moved from the counter. He slowed his steps then, stopped. He looked thoughtfully as he turned about and started back to the front door.

He gave an absent, acknowledging nod to the desk clerk as he passed.

The desk clerk nodded in response. "Good evening, Sergeant," he said.

Alan hesitated, looked curiously back at the unlocked door of William's loft as he slowly closed it. He looked into the room again. Soft evening light was glowing a dull yellow through the wall of windows and into room.

The damage that had been done was still evident, though much of the previous disarray and destruction had been straightened up. Security cameras were working, the monitors creating a brighter glow in that part of the loft. They were displaying the stairwell, hall and alley.

Valerie was sitting on the couch.

Alan walked a wide circle around the loft, Valerie watching.

"What happened here?" he asked.

"William may have gone too far," she stated flatly.

"They took him away?"

"I expect he's gone into hiding."

Alan reached the table, sat on the corner and looked across at Valerie.

"All right," he said. "I doubt his disappearance is why I'm here."

"Might be related."

There was an awkward silence in the loft that lasted for several long moments.

Alan folded his arms across his chest. "He's in deeper than even you knew…"

"It would be just like William," Valerie said, the hint of a smile.

"Right," said Alan. There was another long pause. Alan let his gaze drift from Valerie to the wall of windows, slowly back to Valerie. "I had a chance to chat again with Sullivan."

"Yes? And what did our friendly neighborhood detective have to say?"

"This and that." Alan lost his smile then. "So, Valerie… is there someone interested in our activities that I don't yet know about."

"Ah…" Valerie fumbled with her thoughts. She sat forward on the couch.

"And so," Alan stated. "This is why I'm here."

"I may have an idea who Detective Sullivan might be referring to."

She stood then, folded her arms as she stepped away from the couch. Alan watched her move to the wall of windows. She stared out into the early evening.

Alan pushed away from the table. "Uh, huh."

Valerie continued looking out the window, silent. To Alan it was as if she was anxious about something.

"So?" he urged.

Valerie sighed.

"They call themselves the Alliance," she said at last.

"And they are?"

"Company bosses, rich folks, heads of families." She shrugged. "I don't know names. Secret organization, after all."

"And just what is this secret organization about?"

"They're all about surviving in the system, whatever that takes."

Alan thought on that…

"And the city knows about them," he stated. Not a question.

"And they want to bring them down," said Valerie. She turned from the window and looked directly at Alan. "Your friend Cain knows of 'em. He wants a piece of the action; that or remove the competition."

"Action?"

"Smuggling."

"I see. And that's where Richard comes into the picture."

"Maybe," said Valerie. "Where in the picture, I don't know."

Alan struggled to take all this in. This changed things, and created more questions than it answered.

"You're a member of this Alliance?" he asked.

"No... not a member," said Valerie. "I occasionally, rarely, act as an independent contractor."

"Really." This also created more questions, but he decided to let this one go for the moment. Another question, though... "And why haven't I heard of this Alliance before?"

"They tend not to advertise."

"The Mayor and Cain know about them."

"And neither wants the general population to know there's a secret organization working in the shadows of Willow City."

Alan moved up beside Valerie, leaned against the counter.

"All right," he said. "And you chose not to tell me about them until now because...?"

"Come now, Alan," said Valerie. "First you were a high-ranking NCO in the military, their military. Now you're a retired NCO with a very bright spotlight shining on you."

"You don't trust me."

"Nothing to do with me. Recent events have made them nervous. They're an antsy bunch to start."

"I'm just trying to find out what happened to my brother."

Valerie gave a sympathetic smile and a shrug. Alan turned away, looked again about the loft. They must've really trashed the place. He hoped the guy was all right. He looked back again at Valerie. She was watching him.

"Do they know where Richard is?" he asked.

"No one knows where Richard is."

"You know that for sure?"

"From what I see, they want to find him as much as you do."

"Is Richard part of this Alliance?"

"Uh... no. No, I can assure you, Richard is not a member."

The evening was cool and gray, the city quiet. A dark sedan was parked half a block from the alley entrance leading to William's loft. Burke and his partner were sitting in the car, absently observing.

Carl appeared from around the corner and walked up the street toward the alley. He saw the sedan parked inconspicuously nearby and quickly took it for what it was. He lifted the hood of his jacket up over his head and continued up the street, passing the alley entrance.

Back in the loft, Valerie stood near the window, appearing somewhat uneasy. Alan walked from the kitchen sink, glass of water in hand, and stood near the kitchen table. He looked curiously across the loft to Valerie.

"Are you all right?" he asked.

"Yeah. Yeah, I'm fine." She didn't sound all that convincing.

"You don't look fine."

Valerie looked briefly in Alan's direction, back out the window.

"I was expecting someone."

"Oh?" An unsettled tone.

"Don't go jumping out the window," said Valerie. "Nothing to freak on."

"I get enough surprises."

"Yeah, well... he should have been here by now, so... not happening in any case." She moved away from the window. "He must have been held up. No matter. We can meet up with him another time."

"And whom might that be?" asked Alan; still not happy. "Part of the Alliance revelation?"

Valerie looked across to Alan. "I should talk with him first."

§

Sgt. Burke and his partner watched from their sedan as Valerie left the alley and turned up the street. She reached her car a block further up.

They watched then as Alan came out of the alley and started in the opposite direction. He continued on foot until he reached the corner and turned up the next street.

As Burke watched, he absently brushed at the stubble on his cheek with two fingers.

"Didn't take long for Thornton to move in on his brother's lady," he said.

Partner started the car, sneered. "Didn't expect different."

Chapter Eight

John Benton was at his desk, hovering over paperwork and folders, occasionally put pen to paper. He finished then, closed the last folder. He tossed the pen aside and leaned back in his chair. Glancing across at the computer monitor, the desktop screen clock showed 3:40 PM.

Good enough...

He reached over, set his hands to the computer keyboard and struck several keys. He turned off the monitor then, stood up and took the folders to the four-drawer file cabinet. He opened the top drawer and inserted the folders.

He left his office, flipping off the light switch on his way out. He took the narrow back office hallway to the front office of Intercity Trade. He opened the door to the supply closet. He glanced once back behind him before reaching into the closet.

He pulled at a hidden release and the back wall of the closet opened, revealing a staircase beyond. He descended the stairs to an underground room.

Two of the walls were lined with shelves stocked with office supplies. There was a cot set against one bare wall, a narrow horizontal window set high in the wall above the cot. A work counter was set against another wall, cluttered with small boxes and a small backpack.

There was a pallet of boxes near one corner; the labels on the larger boxes identified the contents as paper. Several smaller boxes sitting on the boxes of paper were labeled "ink cartridges, laser printer" and "ink cartridges, inkjet printer".

There was a folding table and one chair in the middle of the room. On the table were the remains of a meal. Next to the plate and glass was a stack of folders, one open and exposing papers.

William Valentine came into the room through a narrow door, the only other access to the room. He looked over at Benton as he returned to the table.

"John," he sat down, grabbed a half-eaten roll and took a bite as he pulled the open folder nearer. He spoke without looking at Benton. "Where's the computer I asked for? I need to get online."

"We've been through this," said Benton. "You stay in the dark."

William closed the folder, tossed the last of the roll into his mouth and turned in the chair to face Benton.

"That's not your call," he said.

"Nor yours." Benton moved into the middle of the room. "I just came down to see if you need anything. I'm heading home."

"I'm not a prisoner." William pushed aside his plate and looked up at Benton. "I didn't agree to this."

"Sure you did. You had a choice. I on the other hand did not."

William leaned back in his chair. He looked over at the pallet of paper and ink cartridges, then to Benton.

"They can be very persuasive, at that."

"Yes," Benton sighed. He looked in the direction of William's focus, moved over to the pallet. "Alternatives were non-existent."

He lifted one of the smaller boxes and looked at it... ink cartridges.

"I knew Richard was mixed up in something, of course," he said. He set the box back on the pallet.

"But not the Alliance," said William.

"I never heard of 'em," said Benton. "Oh, I knew there were shady groups out there. This is Willow City after all, but not..."

"Not anything so much a part of the system."

"I don't know what I thought. I just kept my head down and did my job." Benton put on a sad grin as he pushed the box of ink aside. "Guess I should have looked up once in a while."

"Why?"

"Maybe I'd have seen this coming."

"And?"

Benton thought about that, tried to come up with something, but had no answer; not if he was honest with himself.

He moved away from the pallet and returned to the staircase.

"Do you need anything?"

"Computer access."

"Not happening. Your handlers said no."

"I don't work for the Alliance," William insisted.

"So you said. You don't like it, leave." With that, Benton climbed the stairs.

Once alone, William looked down at his plate. He picked up a piece of food and tossed it into his mouth.

A nondescript sedan entered an underground parking garage, traveled down a row to an interior wall. It turned and followed the wall, stopped before an elevator door.

A man in a dark suit stepped out of the front passenger door as a woman stepped out of the rear driver's side door. Neither showed any emotion.

The man went to the elevator as the woman opened the passenger side back door.

Valerie climbed out of the back of the sedan. The woman escort indicated the elevator door. Valerie approached as the man escort slid a key card into a slot on the wall beside the elevator. The indicator light turned green. Moments later, the door slid open.

The three entered the elevator car. The man pressed a button and the door slid closed.

§

Valerie entered an understated office, the woman escort entering behind her and moving silently to one side.

A tall, slender man dressed in tailored slacks and button shirt was standing behind a large, simple desk, his back to the desk. He was facing a wall of windows, his hands clasped behind his back.

He turned slowly about to face Valerie. The Alliance leader was in his fifties, had the look and air of calm confidence.

"Miss Baker," he said with a slight nod. "It has been a while."

"Yes sir," said Valerie. "Thank you for agreeing to see me."

"Of course." The Alliance leader indicated the guest chair as he moved around his desk. He sits on the front corner of the desk, waited for her to sit down. "I understand you are seeking information."

"I'm looking for someone," said Valerie.

The Alliance leader raised a questioning brow, waited for Valerie to continue.

"William Valentine," said Valerie.

"And what makes you think I can help you in locating this William Valentine?"

"I believe you know where he is."

"Is that so?"

"Only the Alliance would be hiding him," said Valerie. "Process of elimination."

"I see," said the Alliance leader. "William Valentine, you say?"

"I admit, I don't know why you would hide him," said Valerie. "In the grand scheme of things, William isn't all that important."

"It would appear that he is important to you."

"I just want to know that he's all right."

The Alliance leader stood, moved around to the leather chair behind his desk. He sat and scooted forward.

"A friend of yours," he said calmly.

Valerie didn't answer. The answer was obvious.

The Alliance leader managed a smile.

"A friend of mine, as well," he said.

"Is he?" Valerie hadn't expected that.

"Yes, ma'am." He set his elbows on the desk, looked at his hands, intertwined his fingers. "What do you think of our friend's journalistic skills, Miss Baker?"

"They will get him disappeared one day," she answered quickly, confidently. "If they haven't already."

"I too believe he has talent." The Alliance leader's tone grew more somber. "His endeavors have drawn the ire of one; how William acquires his information however, is both the desire and the threat of many."

"Is he a threat to the Alliance?"

The Alliance leader slid his arms off the desk as he leaned back in his chair. He gave a subtle signal to the woman escort standing to one side. She took a step forward as the Alliance leader looked again to Valerie.

"William is under our protection," he said matter-of-factly.

The escort took another step forward. The Alliance leader nodded sharply; a sign that the meeting was at an end.

Valerie rose from the guest chair. She followed the escort to the door, stopped then and looked back to the Alliance leader.

"Richard Thornton?" she asked.

The Alliance leader put on a thin smile.

"Not the doing of the Alliance, Miss Baker."

The sun was just setting, dusk was on the way. The limo driver stepped quickly around the black limousine that had stopped at the sidewalk in front of Cain's Club. He looked vigilantly about. Seeing no threats, he opened the passenger side back door of the vehicle.

Arthur Cain stepped out. He spoke dismissively to the driver.

"That'll be all this evening."

The driver closed the back door as Cain walked to the front door of the club.

Inside, the sound of bluesy jazz was playing quietly in the background, coming from hidden speakers placed strategically throughout the club.

The security man was in the lobby. He stepped back and out of the way. Cain ignored him as he passed through the lobby and entered the club proper. Less than half the tables and booths were occupied. The sound of muffled voices mixed with the blues music.

Cain walked across the floor, greeted several guests with a quick hello or a pat on the shoulder as he worked his way across the room. Rather than going to his private table, he approached a booth where Alan was sitting alone, a glass of iced tea in hand.

Cain slid into the booth opposite Alan.

"Good evening, Alan," he said. "Good of you to drop by."

Alan lifted his glass in response, set the tea back on the table without taking a drink.

"I appreciate the invitation," he said. "I understand you have news."

"Information," said Cain, after a long pause. "It is for you to determine whether or not it is news."

A waitress approached the table with a glass of water. Cain leaned back as she placed the glass on the table and departed.

Cain shifted on the padded booth bench, rested his arms on the table and held the water glass in both hands.

"Richard... your brother... well, let's just say that he pretty much stumbled his way into the gray market."

"Okay," said Alan. "No news there."

Cain looked up from his water. There was no humor on that face.

"You understand... he is of little value on his own. It is rather his connections to the network."

"These connections, is that what you're after?"

"For a start," said Cain. "Such would potentially offer inroads into a market that I have long sought access to."

"Smuggling," said Alan. "Ink?"

Cain smiled briefly, took a long breath.

"That particular product was why the city-state was interested in your brother," said Cain. "They already control the Internet. Take out the network that is bringing in paper and ink, and they control the majority of the underground information market."

"They had Richard," said Alan. "And lost him."

"Embarrassing, to say the least," said Cain. He took a drink from his glass of water. "Which presents a suitable segue... since the city-state is actively seeking your brother, then they don't know where he is. And, as I also do not know where he is... who does that leave?"

"The Alliance?"

"Very good, Mr. Thornton. That was my thought as well." Cain took a long breath. "Alas, no."

"No? Then who?"

"Ah. Therein the information that I provide." Cain leaned forward. "I offer the question. If not the city and not the Alliance, is there someone new in the picture?"

Chapter Nine

Carl was at his piano, casually working at the keys; light piano jazz. A cigarette was burning in the ashtray on the piano near him. Next to the ashtray was a glass of water with a slice of lemon.

The evening had yet to get started; less than half the tables were occupied. Bonnie was moving about the floor, stopping at one and then another table to give a friendly hello to the customers.

She returned to the stage, leaned against the piano. She took a drag from his cigarette, returned it to the ashtray.

Carl stopped his playing. There were a few quiet hand claps from the audience as he took a drink from his water.

"Slow start," he said. "Quiet crowd."

"Don't sweat it." Bonnie was looking out across the audience floor. "First set isn't for half an hour."

Carl took another drag from his cigarette and put it back in the ashtray.

"Recurring nightmare," he said, again tickling the keys. "I come out one night and no one shows up."

"Oh, never fear, brother. I'll always be here. And I know Eddie would never miss the show."

"I feel reassured." Carl let his gaze drift then across the audience as he continued to absently work the keys. "Nothing from Valerie," he said then.

"Did you expect Miss Harper to come rushing back to give you the good news?"

"I did. I absolutely did." Carl ran the keys, stopped and reached for his cigarette. He took a last drag, put out the butt. He returned to the keys. "I expect she's chasing down whatever news they gave her."

Bonnie smirked. "How rude of her."

Carl gave a knowing smile, refocused on the keys. Bonnie turned about, looked out across the club.

"Or they disappeared her," she said with a sigh. "But at least then she'll know where William is."

Alan was sitting on one of the couches in the Veterans Center lounge. It was late, he was alone. He was only half paying attention to the display on the monitor. It was showing the mayor returning to Willow City. He was walking across a tarmac from his personal jet to a limousine, his spouse several paces behind. The mayor waved to a small crowd standing behind a barrier as a security man opened the rear door of the limo.

Valerie entered the lounge and sat on the couch next to Alan. The two watched the monitor in silence for a few moments. Alan looked side-glance once at Valerie, continued watching the monitor and waited for her to initiate the conversation.

Valerie spoke then, eyes on the display.

"I have news. And I have... what's the opposite of news?"

On the monitor, the display showed the limo leaving the tarmac.

Alan ignored Valerie's question.

"The mayor didn't look happy," he said.

The mayor entered his office foyer. One dim light faintly illuminated the room. Being evening, the receptionist desk was unoccupied.

The mayor walked to his office door.

The overhead light of his office was on. Walking across to his desk, he glanced over at Chief Archer, who was waiting in one of the chairs set against the wall.

Archer stood and walked across the room as the mayor moved in behind his desk. The mayor sat down, indicating the guest chair.

Archer sat.

"I trust your trip went well," he said.

"Such trust is misplaced, Archer."

"I'm sorry to hear that, Mayor."

The mayor grumbled and looked aside.

"If the ball wasn't bad enough, and it was ghastly, it was the pull-aside with our president that truly made the trip dreadful." The mayor turned his focus on his police chief. "The Federation knows far too much of Willow City's day to day, Archer. I don't like it. I don't like it one damn bit."

"What did the president have to say, sir?"

"Enough to tell me that he knows what's working and what isn't, and he enjoys letting me know as much." The mayor wore a darker frown then. "We look less than sparkling in Federation eyes."

"Yes sir," Archer said hesitantly. "Sir, we've known all along the Federation has eyes and ears in the city."

"I fear something much more organized than just a few moles." The mayor stared coolly across the desk. "And more than that, I fear where this might be leading."

Archer suspected where the mayor was going with that thought.

"The city-states are fully autonomous, Mr. Mayor," he said. "Any Federation interference in the internals of one would risk reprisals from all."

"The president is a sly one, Archer. What interference he might take would be subtle, yet effective."

"Yes sir," said Archer.

The mayor leaned back in his chair, grew thoughtful. He brought his hands together, steepled his fingers.

"Question one..." he began. "What would be the purpose of this interference? The action must serve to benefit the Federation directly, perhaps the president indirectly."

He paused then, let that first question settle in the mind.

"Question two..." he continued. "What form would such interference take? This would depend on the purpose."

"Did your pull-aside with the president provide any clues as to the purpose?" asked Archer.

The mayor pulled his hands apart, leaned forward and slid his forearms onto his desk.

"What news of Richard Thornton, Chief Archer?" he asked.

Archer hesitated, considered the sudden redirection...

No, not a redirection. The Thornton matter must have come up in the pull-aside with the president.

"Mr. Mayor... while we have yet to locate Thornton, our investigation suggests that neither Cain nor the Alliance is responsible for his disappearance."

"He could not have eluded us on his own," said the mayor. "He had to have had help."

"I agree."

The mayor looked critically at Archer. "And has his brother been of benefit to your investigation?"

"Not as of yet, Mr. Mayor."

"Then I want him gone," the mayor said darkly. "I want Master Sergeant Thornton erased, and then I want him gone."

The taxi pulled up to the curb just as Alan came out of the veterans center, the sun just beginning to burn off an early morning mist. He climbed into the back seat and slipped his ID card into the reader.

He waited then, ready to pull out the card.

After too many seconds, the indicator light turned red instead of green.

Alan looked to the driver. The driver looked back at Alan through the rearview mirror. He said nothing. He took no action whatsoever. He waited.

Alan pulled his card from the reader and climbed out of the taxi. He stood on the sidewalk then, watched the cab pull away from the curb and drive down the street. He noticed then a black sedan parked nearby... almost as if it was waiting for him.

He approached the sedan. Detective Sullivan was sitting in the rear passenger seat, the window rolled down.

"Good morning, Alan," said Sullivan. "Problem?"

Alan gave a thin smirk as he looked up and down the street. The gray mist was continuing to burn away, the day growing brighter.

He walked around the car and climbed into the back seat beside Sullivan. The driver started the vehicle and started up the street.

Sullivan looked over at Alan, grinned then and focused on the street ahead.

"I'll see what I can do about clearing your ID," he said.

"Archer's doing?" asked Alan.

"Probably," said Sullivan. The initiator field had listed "city-state", which was the default value when a new record was added to the database.

He looked directly at Alan, then.

"It was going to happen, sooner or later," he said. "The timing suggests they're looking to push you down a path of their choosing."

"I'll choose my own path, all the same to you," said Alan.

"Sure." Sullivan looked out his side window, watched the passing scene for a few moments. "Whatever the reason for bringing your brother in that night, however they lost him, most thought him dead soon after."

"But no longer?"

"They've been following your every move since you came into town, hoping you'll lead them to him," said Sullivan. "So someone thought he might still be alive."

"Are you saying that's changed?"

"Your brother being alive? Don't know. Not what I'm suggesting." Sullivan turned from the side window to look at Alan. "Maybe the mayor has run out of patience; maybe he's feeling pressured. But they're no longer looking for you to lead them to Richard."

Sullivan waited then, watched for some sign that Alan understood what that meant. Alan in turn looked away from Sullivan, turned to the view beyond his own side window.

"Right," he said.

"Not so good for you," said Sullivan.

"Right," Alan said again.

The vehicle came to a stop in from of Sally's.

Sullivan nodded in the direction of the café.

"Join me for breakfast?" he asked. "I'm buying."

"I appreciate the offer, but no thanks."

"Other plans?"

"I've eaten."

Sullivan gave a slow nod, laid a hand on the handle and opened his door. "You watch yourself, Alan."

"I'll do that."

Sullivan looked to the driver. "Take Sergeant Thornton wherever he wants to go."

The driver looked at those in the back through the rearview mirror. He nodded once.

Sullivan slid out of the car. He leaned back in, one hand on the door, the other on the roof of the car.

"Alan... this is Willow City. There are always interests working in the shadows. There are sides hidden in sides, hidden in sides."

"And what side might you be on, Sullivan?" asked Alan.

Sullivan lifted his gaze, looked up and down the street, looked back to Alan with a slight, sad, knowing expression.

"I walk a path to a better Willow City, my friend." He leaned down, looked in to the driver. "Back for me in an hour."

Sullivan straightened and closed the door. He gave the roof of the vehicle two pats with the palm of his hand, then watched the sedan pull away from the curb.

He turned and looked into the café. A few of the booths were occupied, and most of the stools at the counter.

He smiled in anticipation and started to the front door.

Chapter Ten

Alan used the remote to turn off the monitor, walked across his vet cen room to the accompanying sound of knocking on the door. Opening the door, Sgt. Burke and his partner stood out in the hall.

"Good evening, Sergeant Thornton." Burke moved into the room, his partner following, forcing Alan to step aside.

"Doesn't Sullivan ever take time off?" asked Alan. He had just seen Sullivan that morning; early that morning.

Sgt. Burke put on a menacing grin, said nothing.

"Sullivan?" Partner snickered.

Alan looked curiously from one to the other of the officers. "Oh. I see."

He took the two steps over to the desk chair, took his jacket from the back of the chair. Holding his jacket in one hand, he casually opened the desk drawer.

The revolver wasn't there.

Doing his best to maintain calm, he slowly closed the drawer, turned from the desk.

"Shall we?" He put on his jacket as he led the way to the open door.

Sgt. Burke wore the hint of a grin as he glanced briefly at the desk, then followed the others out of the room.

Reaching the first floor, Sgt. Burke and his partner escorted Alan across the lobby, passing the front counter on their way to the front door. The desk clerk came in from a back room and stood at the counter.

"Good evening, Sergeant Thornton," he said.

Alan gave a friendly nod, said nothing.

Sgt. Burke ignored the desk clerk; his partner coldly eyed the man as they passed the front desk.

The desk clerk waited for them to leave the center, then reached down and pick up the heavy receiver of the phone that was hidden behind the counter. He dialed a number from memory.

Sgt. Burke assisted Alan into the back seat of the sedan parked at the curb, followed him in. Partner slid in behind the wheel and started the vehicle.

It was early evening, the quiet streets near-empty. Burke eyed Alan, looked ahead, again looked to the Alan.

"Just curious, Thornton," he said. "Just what did you hope to accomplish, bumbling about in the dark?"

Alan said nothing, watched the passing scene, the empty streets, the shimmering walls of the buildings, damp from an increasing fog.

"I mean, did you really think you'd find anything?" asked Burke. "You some great detective?"

Alan continued to hold his silence, to watch the scene beyond the window.

Sgt. Burke reached into a pocket and brought out an old revolver... Alan's revolver, the revolver that had disappeared from the desk drawer in Alan's room.

"And just what did you expect to do with this?" Burke held the revolver in his lap. He grinned. "Yeah, we dropped by your room earlier."

Alan looked down at the revolver, quickly looked away, again out his window.

"You understand..." Burke said in a heavy sigh, "these are so, so not allowed in a peaceful society such as ours."

Alan kept his focus outside the sedan. "So what happens now?"

Sgt. Burke didn't answer.

Partner turned the vehicle off the street and down into the police station parking garage. He steered the vehicle down one row, down a ramp to the next level, parked then in an isolated area of the parking garage.

Sgt. Burke urged Alan out with a sharp nod of the head. The partner took his arm and escorted him around to stand beside Burke.

Alan looked about at their isolation. Several parked vehicles, no one around. A dull-colored wall twenty feet away, an elevator door, a card reader on the wall beside the door.

"Is this where I get disappeared?" he asked.

Sgt. Burke appeared slightly amused by the question.

"Oh, that will happen, and we have begun taking the necessary steps to get us to that result..."

"I'm sensing a but."

"You see," said Burke. "We realized early on that in your case a simple disappearance would create static that we would have to deal with. Most annoying. Therefore..."

Sgt. Burke paused very briefly as he brought out the revolver and calmly shot his partner in the man's shoulder. The sound of the gunshot echoed throughout the garage.

Burke continued then.

"... we first need to establish the circumstances necessary to take us where we need to go."

Partner fell back, stumbled as he grabbed his shoulder, dropped to his knees.

"What the—" Partner fumbled, burbled, "Burke..."

"Stop whining. You'll live." Burke looked then to Alan as he put the revolver back into his pocket, pulled his own pistol from its holster. He put on a mock frown. "Damn. He sure did a lousy job of frisking you. How the hell did he miss a big, bad gun on your person, Thornton?"

"Now you just shoot me?"

"Oh, God no. There would be way too many questions. First we take you upstairs. Then we disappear you in plain sight. Then we shoot you."

Burke looked unceremoniously at his partner.

"Get up," he said. To Alan, then, indicating the elevator door with a wave of his weapon. "Let's go. Archer is waitin' on us."

They stepped past Partner as he struggled to get to his feet. Partner stumbled to follow them, blood oozing through his fingers pressed to his shoulder.

Sgt. Burke brought out a key card and inserted it into the reader next to the elevator. The indicator turned green.

At that moment came the loud, echoing sound of screeching tires. Another moment and two vehicles appeared: a dark sedan followed by a black shiny van.

The side door of the van slid open and four figures wearing black body armor and black masks jumped out and rushed Alan, Burke and his partner.

The elevator door hadn't yet opened.

Sgt. Burke fired his weapon at the nearest masked man, the bullet striking him square in the chest. It barely slowed him down. The two went hand-to-hand, the attacker with a stunner in hand.

A second attacker reached Burke's partner, who was unable to fight back, pressed his own stunner against Partner's chest and pulled the trigger.

The elevator door slid open. Partner was shoved into the car, collapsed to the floor.

Another attacker reached Alan, grabbed him by the arm and rushed him to the waiting sedan.

Sgt. Burke and his attacker continued to struggle. Burke was finally stunned; the attacker took one arm as the fourth attacker took his other. They half dragged Burke to the elevator and shoved him in. They backed away then as the elevator door closed.

Alan was pushed unceremoniously into the sedan; his face planted into the back seat. The door was slammed shut and the vehicle started away as Alan struggled about and sat up.

Detective Sullivan was in the back seat next to Alan. He looked forward.

"Good evening, Mr. Thornton."

The vehicle left the garage, turned onto the street. Behind them, the black van turned in the opposite direction.

"Sullivan." Alan rubbed at a sore arm. "So, where are we going?"

"Safe house."

Alan stood in the middle of a small living room. Sullivan looked into the bedroom, then poked his head into the open door of the bathroom. All clear. He moved then to a window, stood beside it and looked out onto the street below.

Alan watched, looked disinterestedly about the simply furnished apartment.

"Are you Alliance?" he asked.

"Alliance?" Sullivan turned from the window, shook his head no. "Consider this a rare apex where we and the Alliance have a common objective."

"And what might that objective be? Me *not dead*?"

Sullivan managed a light chuckle at that.

"You are a nuisance to both, my friend," he said. "And to just about everyone else. Then, I'm thinking that was what you were going for."

Alan said nothing, looked for Sullivan to give him more.

Sullivan continued. "You dead or disappeared, most would breathe a lot easier."

"Then why the timely rescue? And who the hell are you?"

Sullivan considered his answer, handed Alan the apartment key card as he started toward the door.

"If forced to take a side... Federation." He opened the door. "I'll pick you up in the morning. Important meeting, first thing."

Late evening, the old veteran was alone in the Veterans Center lounge, sitting in one of the easy chairs, watching the television broadcast on the monitor.

Displayed on the screen, the woman newscaster was sitting at the news desk.

"Welcome to the Late Night edition of Truth in Reporting, a service of the National Education Office," she said.

The Veterans Center desk clerk came into the lounge, coffee cup in hand. He sat on the arm of one of the couches. He took a sip of his coffee and watched the program with the old veteran.

The screen behind the newscaster displayed the image of a city street, a number of uniformed men and women forcibly gathering a smaller group of dissidents and shoving them toward the back of a police wagon. Several other dissidents were being forced to remove posters from a brick wall.

The woman newscaster was speaking: "The city-state completed another sweep last evening, removing a number of unsavories from our streets."

The old veteran grumbled.

"Thereby making the city safe for all," he said sarcastically.

"More volunteers for military service," said the desk clerk. Another sip of his coffee.

On the screen, the image behind the newscaster displayed a battlefield, smoke drifting across the landscape. Soldiers were marching across the field.

"It won't always be so, Sergeant," said the old veteran.

The desk clerk continued watching the monitor.

"We shall be the change, Major," he said.

Chapter Eleven

A quiet side street lined with townhouses. Early morning, the sun just coming up.

Alan closed the door of one of these townhouses, took the steps down to the sidewalk and to the open back door of the dark sedan. He climbed in beside Detective Sullivan and closed the door.

Sullivan waited for the vehicle to pull away from the curb before saying anything.

"You slept well?" he asked. Alan.

"Fine, thanks," said Alan. "My first safe house."

"Stayed there myself, once."

Alan looked curiously at Sullivan, quickly decided not to ask... he looked at the passing scene as they turned onto a main thoroughfare.

"Where are we headed?" he asked.

Sullivan looked to the driver, who looked back through the rearview mirror.

"I told you last night," he said then. "We're meeting with someone who may be able to help."

"Yeah, I got that," said Alan. "You were rather light on specifics."

Sullivan looked briefly again to the driver, then out a side window.

"I hear ya," he sighed.

"Uh, huh." Alan looked curiously from Sullivan to the driver, back to Sullivan. "Right."

They turned down another street, drove past brick-walled buildings. Posters haphazardly pasted on the walls reflected resistance to the city-state, highlighted the oppression of the administration and policies, encouraged taking a stand, fighting back, resisting authoritarianism.

The car turned into an open-air parking area next to a small warehouse complex. They pulled into a space near the warehouse side door. A plain sign above the door read "Marshall Distributing".

Inside, the driver led Sullivan and Alan along a hallway, passing several closed doors. He stopped at one, knocked twice, hesitated, then opened the door.

Mrs. Marshall entered her office through a side door as the driver escorted Alan and Sullivan in from the hallway. At sixty years old, she was a strong woman, which shown in her manner and stand. She was well-dressed in professional slacks and blouse. Her well-combed hair held streaks of gray.

She waved her guests fully into the office.

"Come, come," she said. To the driver then, "Thank you, Steven."

Steven the driver/escort nodded and backed out, closing the door as he left. Mrs. Marshall moved into the middle of the room, held her hand out to Sullivan. They shook hands.

"Detective Sullivan," she said. "I've heard many good things about you. So wonderful to finally meet you."

"Thank you, Mrs. Marshall."

She looked then to Alan, shook his hand as well.

"Mr. Thornton. I'm Amanda Marshall."

"Ma'am," Alan said curtly.

Mrs. Marshall moved around behind her desk, indicated the guest chairs as she sat down. She watched them take the chairs.

"To business, then." She looked to Alan, leaned over the desk and clasped her hands. "I hope you appreciate the risk we're taking, Mr. Thornton; revealing our presence in this way."

"And you are?"

Mrs. Marshall wore a slight smile, a thoughtful smile.

"We represent Federation interests here in Willow City."

"And you would prefer that these interests, and your presence, remain private."

"Our activities are best served by remaining undisclosed to certain parties."

She caught then Alan looking thoughtfully over at Sullivan, back to Mrs. Marshall.

"Yes," she said. "The Federation footprint in Willow City is small, and our presence highly compartmentalized." Another smile in Sullivan's direction. "As for Detective Sullivan, his has no doubt been a lonely existence, his focus as per Federation interests somewhat isolating."

"I appreciate the importance of our charge here, Mrs. Marshall," said Sullivan.

"Of course. And yet the lack of timely communication has no doubt on occasion been frustrating."

"On occasion."

Mrs. Marshall slid her arms off the desk as she leaned back in her chair. She studied Alan for a long moment.

"What to do with you, Mr. Thornton?"

"Should I be concerned?"

"You misunderstand. Yes, your queries have drawn attention to matters that are incidentally related to Federation interests, but nothing that we can't deal with." She looked thoughtfully at Alan, considered. "No, the issue before us is whether and how to afford you the protection that Detective Sullivan here has advocated."

"And what form might this protection take? I won't be disappeared."

"Mr. Thornton, again you misunderstand." Mrs. Marshall's tone grew firm. "The Federation has no interest in whether you live, die or disappear. What action we choose to take will serve Federation interests, no matter Detective Sullivan's sponsorship... or what wishes you might entertain."

"As you did with my brother?"

"It became necessary to step in when it was clear the city-state intended to use your brother to ascertain the gray market network. Exposure of that network would have threatened discovery of our own."

"The city-state doesn't know of your network?"

"They don't know of our presence at all, beyond the occasional mole or spy that we allow to be known or suspected."

Sullivan reentered the conversation then.

"Mrs. Marshall? The Federation has Thornton?"

"Detective Sullivan," she acknowledged. To both of them then, "Richard Thornton was with us until just under a month ago."

"Is he all right?" asked Alan. "Where is he now?"

"He left our protection of his own accord, and without our knowledge."

"So where is he?"

"I'm sorry, Mr. Thornton."

"You don't know?"

"We believe he has left Willow City, but he has yet to make an appearance in any of the other city-states."

"I see. And once he does?"

"We will ensure that he is not a threat." Mrs. Marshall stated firmly.

"You're not... you won't—"

"No," she stated. "I do not believe that will be necessary."

Well, at least there was that.

Alan sat back in his chair. He looked to Sullivan, back to Mrs. Marshall across the desk.

"And what about me?"

"Yours is a complex circumstance, Mr. Thornton."

"I get that," said Alan. "A lot."

"I do not doubt that," said Mrs. Marshall. "As for the Federation, the light created by your presence in the city-state pushes back the shadows and threatens to expose our own."

"And Federation interests must be protected, which means hush-hush," said Alan. "Got it."

"A quiet word spoken here, a covert action take there, we may be able to dim that light." Mrs. Marshall leaned nearer. "And you will do your part."

"Which is?" Alan asked warily.

"You must cease looking for your brother."

"Mrs. Marshall—" Sullivan started.

"I won't do that," Alan stated firmly.

Mrs. Marshall calmly lifted a hand, two fingers raised. The call for silence. She was clearly used to giving direction and having that direction taken.

She straightened, looked at Alan with purpose.

"It must be clear to all that you no longer have reason to search for your brother."

"Mrs. Marshall, I—"

"Mr. Thornton. Once we have located your brother, we will let you know."

Sullivan looked from Mrs. Marshall to Alan.

"Alan, let them find your brother," he said. "What can you do on your own? He's not even in the city."

"If that is true."

"Your brother is alive, Alan. Take that." Sullivan stood then, looked across the desk to Mrs. Marshall. "I will see that Mr. Thornton does his part."

"Thank you, Detective Sullivan."

Alan looked dubious, but held his silence.

The Alliance leader stood with John Benton and William Valentine in the front office of Intercity Trade. He was looking out the window onto the warehouse floor, where the pallet of paper and ink was being loaded into the back of a box truck.

He turned from the window.

"Thank you for your assistance, Mr. Benton," he said. "We'll be out of your hair in a few minutes."

"Not a problem," said Benton.

The Alliance leader put on a knowing smile.

"Kind of you to say so," he said. He looked to William. "Mr. Valentine. Chief Archer is still interested in speaking with you. He will be until city hall no longer considers you of value."

"And the Alliance?"

"Your threat to the Alliance is being minimized as we speak."

"You mean, as soon as connections that I have to the Alliance are removed, you'll be cutting me loose."

The Alliance leader appeared consoling. "We'll try and do you better, Mr. Valentine."

A young man came into the office from the warehouse, came up beside the Alliance leader.

"We're about ready, sir," he said. "The roads are clear."

"Thank you."

The young man looked to both John Benton and William.

"We're short six ink cartridges," he said, more than a hint of accusation. "Any idea what happened to them?"

"Me?" Benton almost smirked. "This is all new to me. And after today, it's history. I am gone and gone."

The young man looked then to William.

"I expect Richard held onto them," said William.

"The merchandize does not belong to Thornton," said the young man.

William shrugged. "Handlers fee?"

Benton couldn't help but grin.

"Sounds like Richard," he said.

The Alliance leader gave a dismissive nod to the young man, a sign that he should let it go. The man gave a final disapproving frown to Benton and William, turned about and left.

The Alliance leader then looked to the others.

"Mr. Benton, we should be able to help you *be gone*, as you wish." To William then, "Mr. Valentine?"

William shook his head no.

"I have unfinished business here in Willow City.

The Alliance leader gave William an approving smile.

"Very good, Mr. Valentine."

The mayor was at his desk, hovered over paperwork, signing one document and then another. His receptionist stood waiting patiently beside him. Chief Archer was sitting in a nearby guest chair.

The mayor signed a final document. He gathered the papers together and handed them to his receptionist.

"Thank you, Betty," he said. He looked to her then with an afterthought. "Call my wife. I'll be available for lunch, 1:00 PM."

"Yes, Mr. Mayor." The receptionist stepped away from the mayor and left the office.

The mayor leaned back in his chair, swiveled about and looked across his desk to Archer.

"Richard Thornton," he said, prompting his police chief.

"Yes sir. Numerous sources conclude that Thornton is no longer in the city."

"Excuse me. He left the city? Without our knowledge? That is not possible."

"Nonetheless, sir. It appears to be the case."

The mayor grew contemplative, pursed his lips, tapped at his chin.

"Federation fingerprints."

"Perhaps, Mr. Mayor."

The mayor sat up and leaned forward in his chair.

"What of his brother?" he asked.

"His only value, to anyone, was the possibility that he might lead us to Richard. With his brother gone, Alan Thornton is irrelevant."

"And he's still breathing?"

"Sir—"

"I am certain that I asked this issue be dealt with."

"Yes sir," said Archer. "I'll see to it, Mr. Mayor."

The two grew silent. The mayor raised a brow then, a silent suggestion that the meeting was over. Archer got the message. He stood.

"Right away, sir." He turned to leave.

Mayor watched after him, spoke out before Archer reached the door.

"Archer."

Archer stopped and turned. "Sir."

"Archer." The mayor considered for several painfully long moments. "On reflection... let us monitor only. For now."

"Sir?"

"Brother Alan may yet be of value. He may not have found his brother, but his search may have engendered a few network connections of his own. Let us see where they lead."

"Of course, sir," Archer said with an abbreviated nod.

"And keep an eye out," the mayor continued. "I have no doubt the Federation is scurrying about in the shadows."

Archer gave another, affirmative nod of the head. The mayor spun his chair slowly about, his focus to the window.

He didn't look happy.

"I'll not have Federation boots in my city."

Archer gave a final nod, uncertain, looking at the back of the mayor sitting his chair.

He turned and left the office.

Chapter Twelve

Sgt. Burke sat in the front passenger seat of the unmarked police sedan, the vehicle parked across the street from Sally's Café. His new partner was sitting behind the steering wheel.

Burke took a swallow of coffee from a thermos cup, looked across the street to the café, his expression cool and detached. In the café, visible through the window, Detective Sullivan was sitting in a booth, taking a forkful of what was most likely a piece of pie.

What is it with Sullivan and apple pie?

Burke's new partner opened a small paper bag and took out a plastic bag of apple slices. He pulled out a slice, held it out to Burke.

"Sergeant? Apple slice?"

Burke's expression didn't change. His focus on the window of the café didn't change.

He took another swallow of coffee.

"No."

The new partner pulled back the apple slice.

"All right." He bit into the slice of apple. "Honeycrisp."

Sgt. Burke closed his eyes briefly and set his jaw as if pushing back pain. He took a long sigh, continued watching the café.

§

Morning in the Gray Swan. Carl and Bonnie were sitting at the bar, Carl with a glass of water with lemon, Bonnie with a cup of coffee.

Eddie was standing behind the bar opposite the couple. He looked briefly across at Carl, then focused on the cup he was holding in both hands.

"I wouldn't sweat it, Carl," he said. "We'll get through this."

"Evidence to the contrary," grumbled Carl.

"The city's quieting down. Our friends are seeing to that."

"They can't undo the attention that we've gotten over this."

"They're doing nothing to protect us," said Bonnie, her frown darkening. "City finding us out wouldn't be a threat to the Alliance, so what do they care?"

"The Gray Swan will be fine, Bonnie," said Eddie. "We lay low, provide entertainment and a few hours escape to the citizens of Willow City. Just like always."

Valerie came into the club. She walked over to the bar, stood at the counter beside Carl and Bonnie. She said nothing. Eddie poured a cup of coffee and set it in front of her.

"Thanks, Eddie." She held onto the cup, spoke then without looking at the others. "How's things?"

"You tell us," said Bonnie.

"Don't know much." Valerie took a sip of her coffee, set the cup on the counter. "I'm hearing Richard left town."

"He's all right?" asked Bonnie.

"Guess so. Word is, he left town on his own."

"And he didn't tell anyone?" Bonnie struggled to hide a grin. "He didn't tell you?"

"So it would seem." Valerie looked past Bonnie to Carl. "And I hear they're cleaning up the mess his brother's been making."

"I heard that, too," said Carl. "It looks like Alan is safe. For now."

Bonnie shook her head.

"He should take a cue from Richard, leave town while he can," she said.

"Yeah," said Carl. "I don't see that happening."

Valerie moved her cup aside.

"I don't know Alan very well, but he doesn't seem the kind to just walk away, job not done."

"What's left for him to do?" asked Bonnie.

Valerie looked across at Eddie and pointed to her near-empty cup as she answered.

"Don't know," she said. "But it doesn't feel done to me."

Alan stood in the lobby of Cain's Club, arms held out. Cavanaugh watched the security man pat Alan down. Once cleared, Alan followed Cavanaugh into the club.

A woman was behind the bar organizing inventory. Cain was sitting at his table at the back of club, his associate standing discretely to one side. Cain was eating a piece of toast, a juice glass and a small plate on the table in front of him.

He set the toast on the plate and lifted the glass as he looked side-glance at Alan's approach, Cavanaugh moving to one side.

"Good morning, Mr. Thornton." Cain drank from his juice. "Don't you spread sunshine and buttercups wherever you go? I have to say, I'm thoroughly enjoying your visit to our otherwise gloomy city."

"Yours be a smiling face in a crowd of frowns," said Alan.

Cain indicated a chair, spoke again as Alan sat down.

"And is that what brings you here this morning? Longing for a friendly face?"

"I thought I'd check in, see if you've heard anything."

Cain studied Alan's face for a few moments as he toyed with his juice glass.

"You've no doubt heard the same scuttlebutt as I." He took a swallow of juice, studied Alan a moment. "Ah. I see. You come seeking verification."

"Yes sir."

"I am afraid that I cannot. Not yet."

Alan took a moment to process the '*not yet*'.

"I would appreciate any future updates that may come your way," he said then.

"But of course, my friend." Cain said smugly. He gulped down the last of his juice, set the glass gently aside. "I can assume then that you will be honoring us with your presence for a while longer."

"A reasonable assumption."

Alan walked across the garden-like apartment grounds, carrying his duffle, the duffle he had with him when he had first stepped off the train.

Approaching Richard's old apartment, he saw Wanda near the door, leaning against the porch post, her arms folded across her chest.

"Good morning, neighbor," she said, smiling. She unfolded her arms, held out one hand, showing a key card.

"Thank you, Wanda."

Alan took the card, Wanda pushed off the post and stepped to one side.

"True about Richard, then?" she asked. "He left the city?"

"That's the word."

Wanda waited for more. Nothing more came. She took another step away.

"News could have been worse. Right?"

"Absolutely," said Alan. He gave an awkward smile, held up the key card. "Hey, I got an apartment out of it."

Wanda appeared thankful of Alan's weak attempt at humor.

"I'm so pleased," she said. She started away, stopped after a few steps and looked back at Alan. "Lovely having you as a neighbor, Alan."

Alan gave another awkward smile, watched as Wanda turned again and walked away. He looked up at the blue sky then, back to Wanda's receding figure. He looked down at the key card in his hand.

He weighed his duffle, gave a confident half-grin and turned to the front door of his apartment.

end

www.ingramcontent.com/pod-product-compliance
Lightning Source LLC
Chambersburg PA
CBHW022041170626
46808CB00003B/1311